GABRIELLE MARIE KOZAK

Trooper A1

The Purple Blitzkrieg

First published by Ancilla Mariae Publications 2025

Second edition

ISBN (paperback): 978-1-970936-00-1
ISBN (hardcover): 978-1-970936-01-8

Editing by Corinna Meadows
Advisor: Colette Petrizzi

This book was professionally typeset on Reedsy.
Find out more at reedsy.com

For my younger siblings, who had to listen to my reading them my stories for most of our family life.

For my two best friends, who encouraged me, inspired me—and distracted me. As all good friends do.

And in honor of the Blessed Virgin Mary, my Mother.

"Do I remember anything? ... No. I don't. Who am I?"

— Conner Whyte

Contents

prologue

A scream fills the air. The thirteen-year-old boy and his older brother, both talking quietly about school and standing near the back of the line, look up in surprise as the bank doors open and four masked men, clothed in black, stride in with their guns at the ready.

The two brothers tense. The older one is tall and muscular; he has curly, dark brown hair. The younger boy is thin, short, and delicate-looking; his hair is a very light blond, almost white. But their faces make it obvious that they are related. It is the dark, piercing eyes, the sharp cheekbones, the solid chin.

"Nobody move!" one of the men yells to the panicking crowd.

He and another stay behind near the entryway, while the others make their way to the service desks. One of the bank employees, a young lady, hovers her hand over the telephone for an instant. But then she drops her hand noiselessly onto the desk.

One of the thieves by the door gestures with the gun in his hand. "Empty it out now."

The petrified tellers hasten to obey the order. However, a change is coming over the young man, who now finds that he and his brother are behind the spokesperson. It is apparent from his face that he feels he must do something to stop the crime. His hands clench into fists.

Suddenly, without giving the criminals any warning, he jumps the leader, bringing him to the ground. The gun clatters to the tile floor, and the teenager grabs at it in vain with his free hand, but the gangster retrieves it before he does. The older man is stronger, and succeeds in shoving the teenager off himself and getting back up to his feet. But the teenager scrambles up as well, and while the man recovers himself, he makes another desperate attempt to gain control of the gun, grabbing it and trying to wrest it away from the other's grip.

A shot rings out. The other man by the door has fired in reaction to the trouble his friend is having. Gasping, the teenager feels his strength slipping away, and his hold on the weapon loosens. It is lost completely, and he falls heavily to the floor with a choked cry. His younger brother screams.

"Hurry that up!" the tellers are ordered. Swiftly they finish, and the stolen money is swept into a couple of sacks by the henchmen. The four rush to make their exit. Someone calls the police.

The thirteen-year-old is already at his brother's side. His breath comes quick and fast as he tries to stop his brother's bleeding with his jacket. His older brother opens his eyes, and looks at him. The boy's eyes are flooding with tears, but he stares back.

"Be strong, Conner," his brother gasps out. A spasm of pain goes through him, and he goes limp after a moment of rigidity. Conner blinks rapidly, kneeling frozen in shock.

"Ricky?" he chokes.

He feels a hand on his shoulder, and spins around in panic. But it's just a paramedic.

"Hey, kid. Let me get to the victim," she tells him gently, smiling reassuringly. Dazed, Conner moves aside, and watches as she checks on his older brother. Her face falls after only a few moments of medical procedure. "Sorry. He's gone."

Conner stands there in a state of intense shock as his brother is lifted onto a stretcher and carried out the door into an ambulance. His jacket falls off, and drops to the floor near the door. Conner stares at the blue jacket. Part of it has turned purple.

He has stopped crying, overawed by a dim feeling of unreality. This is all a nightmare. He wants desperately to wake up. This isn't real life. These things don't happen. They shouldn't happen. His breath comes quicker and quicker until it sounds like he's running a marathon.

"Kid." It's the paramedic again, and this time she's looking at him and not his brother. "Are you hurt, too? What's your name? He's your brother, right? Where do you live? Come on; you can ride to the hospital with your brother."

He doesn't move or reply. Carefully the paramedic checks him over; but he looks fine. However, the action seems to wake him up, and he murmurs his brother's name. "Ricky."

"Ricky? Your name is Ricky?"

He shakes his head. The paramedic notices in alarm that his very light-colored skin is starting to turn bluish.

"Come on," she orders. "Come to the ambulance."

Conner makes no reaction. She takes his hand, and checks his pulse. But it is too faint to be felt.

"Let's go," she says again, urgently.

The next moment, the paramedic calls loudly for help as the thirteen-year-old collapses in severe shock.

one

THREE YEARS LATER

It was a small, cozy living room. There was a grandfather clock by one of the doors, and pictures of a lakefront on the walls. The room's space was taken up by a coffee table, a couple of armchairs, and a pair of sofas. On one of the sofas sat a teenage boy, who was reading a newspaper.

He was short, with thick hair of an extremely light hue, nearly as pale as his skin. But his eyes were dark, deep and full of expression.

Though the sixteen-year-old looked distinctly fragile, his chin was firm and set. He wore a white uniform shirt, belt, long gray pants, and black school shoes. At his feet was his backpack. He had just gotten home from school, it appeared.

His eyes moved back and forth as he scanned the newspaper, but then he apparently found an article of interest.

He spread the paper out on his lap, and bent down, moving his fingers along the words as he read them, not just mentally but with his lips, albeit silently.

The sound of the door opening startled him, and he literally jumped, looking up instantly with the expression of one caught in something. But the expression vanished almost right away, before his mother looked at him. She was tall, and a brunette. She wore a work uniform, and carried her purse with her. Glancing at the boy on the couch, she smiled.

"What's up, Conner?"

Conner quickly turned some of the pages of the newspaper, pretended to read for a moment, then shoved the newspaper off his lap onto the coffee table with an expression of nonchalance. "Uhh...nothing really."

"Where's Moira?" Mrs. Victoria Whyte asked next, walking through the living room on her way to her bedroom.

Conner shut his eyes for a moment. "She had something to do after school, I guess...she's not home. Oh. Now she is," he added, upon hearing the front door open and close.

"I'm home!" a young girl's voice rang out cheerfully. She entered the living room a moment later. "Hello, Mom. Hey, Conner."

"Hello, Moira," Victoria smiled. "Don't forget to change out of your uniform."

"I won't," the girl assured her mother.

She was Conner's twin sister, but unlike him in almost every way. She was much taller, and she was a light brunette. Her skin might have been as white as his at some point, but now it was colored by a healthy tan. Everything about her spoke strength and quick-wittedness, including her practical way of holding back her bobbed hair with a single, plain clip. Her school outfit was a white blouse, green skirt, navy blue tights, and—well, after the above, one would have expected neat, dignified shoes. But Moira wore sneakers. And the white sleeves of her shirt were smudged, most likely with dirt.

The mother left the room, but Conner's voice stopped Moira when she was halfway to the hall.

"How was volleyball?" he asked her.

She grinned. "It was great."

"Did you win?" Conner followed up.

"Actually, it was a tie. But Cloe wasn't there, and she's our best, so I'm not surprised," Moira told him. Sensing that he wanted to start a conversation, she made her way across the room and dropped her backpack onto the coffee table with a sigh of relief. "Have you started homework yet?" she inquired, before noticing the newspaper. "Or just the news?"

Conner looked up at her. "Yeah...just reading the news," he admitted.

Moira was very perceptive, and couldn't help but notice the look on his face. "What's wrong?"

"There was a bank robbery yesterday," Conner replied shortly, keeping eye contact. "On the other side of the city."

The two pairs of dark eyes stared into each other, their look full of meaning.

"It was three years ago, Conner," Moira murmured. "There can't possibly be a connection."

Conner dropped his gaze to the floor. "But what if there is?"

"Conner, this isn't the first time it's happened since. What strikes you about this one?" Moira asked, sitting down next to him and picking up the paper.

She flipped through the pages and scanned each one briefly until she found what Conner had been so interested in: an article on the bank robbery, complete with a witness's narration of the crime.

Conner watched her as she read it. "See the description?" he asked. "It matches what... I saw," he finished dully, swallowing hard and looking away from her.

"Don't hoodlums dress and act the same?" his twin muttered, shoving the newspaper aside and putting her feet up on the coffee table.

"I think they usually wear black," Conner replied, adding: "But this time, dark gray."

Moira gesticulated uselessly for a moment before finding words. "But how can it be connected? Maybe these ones just...didn't like black?"

"But how likely is it that they'd have the same style of clothes?" Conner returned.

Moira considered for a moment before shrugging. She glanced at her brother, but he was still looking away from her. "What're you gonna do?"

"I dunno," Conner murmured. "Probably nothing."

"Then—" Moira began.

"Forget it," Conner broke in, standing up. "It was just a theory."

"Hey, some theories are correct," Moira pointed out, rising in turn.

Conner turned and looked at her. "Yeah?"

"Yeah. Like my theory that you aren't going to do nothing," Moira countered, grinning. "So what are you going to do?"

Conner shrugged, picked up his backpack, and headed for the door. "I'm going to finish homework. And then I'm going to take a walk."

two

The bank at which the latest robbery had taken place was already back to normal. There was the ordinary line of customers, and the usual employees in their usual uniforms. But a young man in his mid-teens who inconspicuously entered the bank wasn't looking for any of that. In fact, it would have been hard to determine exactly what he *was* looking for. He took a few steps past the door, looked around the interior of the building, and stepped right back out and walked down the street. For all any of the onlookers could have known, it might as well have been simple curiosity.

The same boy who had performed the momentary pop-in now walked at a moderate pace down the street. Actually, it looked like he was trying to hurry, but his thin legs didn't do much to help. But he stopped short and looked behind him when he heard his name shouted.

"Conner!"

Conner obviously recognized the boy: a brown-haired, tanned-skinned, casually dressed young man who was almost a head taller than he was.

Conner's face broke into a grin, and he turned to meet the newcomer.

"Jack!" he exclaimed.

"Hey, Conner," Jack Marwick replied, catching up to Conner and falling in line. "'Sup?"

"Nothing, I'm just walking," Conner told him. "What about you?"

"Mom wants me to get something from the store," Jack explained. "Wanna come?"

"Sure," Conner responded.

"How's homework coming?" Jack inquired. "Did you finish?"

"I haven't started," Conner admitted, flushing.

Jack laughed. "Me neither. But I'm a procrastinator."

Conner grinned. "At least tomorrow's Friday."

"Yikes, don't talk about the weekend," Jack muttered. "We've got a lot of those still before the next break." But then his face brightened up visibly. "We're gonna do some shooting on Saturday, though. Wanna come?"

"Got enough ear protection?" Conner asked, laughing.

Jack nodded emphatically. "Yup."

"I'm game," Conner declared.

* * *

"Hey, what are all you guys doing for the weekend?" Moira asked some friends the next afternoon on the volleyball court. Moira and her best friend were tossing the volleyball back and forth. One of their other team members was over by the net, talking to her older sister, who was on the other team; the other two members of Moira's team were watching the tossing game, one of them drinking out of her water bottle.

Lucinda Montoya laughed, making a neat catch and throwing the ball back to Moira. "Nothing special. We're having a barbecue on Sunday, I think."

One of the other two was going on a weekend vacation to Washington; the other was also doing "nothing special."

"Cloe!" Moira shouted to the girl at the net, who turned around.

"What?" she demanded. Clotilde Marwick was a short, dark brown-haired girl of fifteen, and the girl on the other side of the net was her twenty-three-year-old sister Nina.

"What are you doing for the weekend? Swimming? Studying?" Moira repeated, trying to catch Lucinda off guard by tossing the ball at the same time she was talking. But Lucinda caught it nevertheless and hammered it back in playful revenge.

"Actually, we're driving into northern Virginia," Nina replied for her sister.

"For a party," Cloe added, grinning.

"Haha, sounds fun," Moira laughed.

"Whose party?" Lucinda wanted to know.

"The Dal Bellos' house," Nina supplied.

Their conversation was interrupted by the arrival of Moira's twin, who came walking behind the school building. Moira saw him, and waved. Waving back with a big grin on his face, he sat himself down on a bench by the court.

"I'm here for the game," Conner yelled. "What's up? Am I too late?"

"No," Moira shouted, "we're waiting for Christina."

It was then that Nina's phone began ringing. She yelled at two of her teammates to stop singing scales so she could answer the call. Moira feinted a toss to Lucinda before actually throwing it as Lucinda protested vehemently; next followed some hard, rapid volleys. Both of the girls were efficient at the game of catch, and gradually they backed up until they were throwing from a distance of about fifteen yards. The bright spring sun beat down on them both, and on everyone else except Cloe, who got into some shade afforded by the supply shed. Conner pulled the hood of his jacket down as low as it would go over his face to shield himself.

"Aren't you hot in that?" Moira shouted, glancing his way momentarily before returning the ball to Lucinda.

"It's better than burning the skin off my face," Conner called back, his voice muffled.

Moira shrugged, and continued the game with her friend. "Really, if I didn't know your family I'd never believe that you two were twins," Lucinda commented in a low voice.

"Yeah?" Moira returned, keeping her eyes on the ball as Lucinda did a few feints in an attempt to catch her off guard.

"Yeah," Lucinda echoed. "You're everything he isn't. You're agile, fast, and strong; he's weak. Your skin can take the sun; his burns in seconds. Your hair is dark; his is super li—"

"Just throw it," Moira interrupted, getting impatient. Laughing, Lucinda obliged with a hard, straight shot. Moira caught it, stepping back a bit to deflect the impact. She was about to show her friend how to *really* throw when Nina got off the phone.

"Christina can't come," she announced dolefully, dropping her cellphone into her pocket. "You guys wanna reschedule?"

"Blast," Cloe muttered.

"Nah," Moira told Nina. "Let's just play."

"We're short one player," Nina pointed out dryly. "It's not even."

Moira shrugged. "Dora, if you play with them today, Conner can play with us."

"You're kidding, right?" Lucinda hissed as one of their team glanced sideways at Moira, shrugged, and ducked under the net to the other side.

Moira shook her head. "Any objections?"

Her other four teammates were too polite to say they didn't want to play on a team with Conner, though they knew full well that he was incapable of playing any sport, and that he'd only get in their way. So Moira met with no opposition.

"Conner!" she yelled, turning to face the bench some distance away.

The figure on the bench raised his hooded head an inch or so. "Yeah?" His voice was less muffled than it had been before.

"Wanna play?"

three

"You remember how to play, right?" Moira was asking her twin a few seconds later. He'd gotten off the bench and walked onto the volleyball court, pushing his jacket hood back.

Now he smiled tentatively. "Are you sure about this? I'll lose the game on you."

"You can't lose forever," Moira laughed. "You'll get lucky sometime."

Conner didn't look too sure of that, but obligingly he took up a stand in the center of their side of the court, where Lucinda directed him. No one on Moira's team looked too confident, but they were going to try their best. Meanwhile, Nina grinned and set her own team up.

"Moira, you're serving first," Lucinda called out. Moira darted over to serving position, with the ball.

"Play by time or by score?" Nina shouted.

Feeling small in the center of their half of the volleyball court, Conner flexed, trying to prepare himself for the action he knew was coming. Just as soon as the game started.

"Score!" Lucinda, the captain of the team Moira was on, decided. "Fifteen."

"Here goes a flunk," Moira heard Conner mutter. She stopped bouncing the ball and turned to look at him. He shaded his eyes with his hand to look back at her.

"Chin up, trooper, and let's go crush this," she grinned. Conner grinned back, a half-hearted grin that didn't take over his face like Moira's did hers. But it was good enough for his energetic, optimistic twin.

"Are we playing?" someone called impatiently from the opposing team.

Lucinda, playing behind Moira, tapped her shoulder. "Come on! Let's start!"

* * *

"This makes fourteen!" Nina yelled triumphantly about twenty minutes later, as the ball hit the ground just beyond Moira's desperate slide and rolled away almost nonchalantly. Lucinda ran after it.

Moira's outfit was dustier than it had ever gotten, which actually said a lot, and she was panting. She wanted so much to win this game and prove to Conner that it could be done. "You're only one point ahead," she gasped out.

"Conner, it's your turn to serve," Lucinda announced, tossing the ball to him.

Conner's hands flew out in an effort to catch the ball. It flew through them and into his stomach, knocking the air out of him before rolling down to the ground. Quickly he bent down and grabbed it, getting into serving position. He hesitated, his left hand doubling into a fist and his right hand holding the ball ready. Tentatively he swung his left hand.

"Don't be scared of hitting it," Moira yelled, brushing herself off. "Hit it with all you've got. Hard! Swing faster—! YEAH!"

There was the dull sound of Conner's fist striking the ball; then a faint whistle, or more of a rushing sound, as it sailed over the net. One of Nina's team bumped it back, swift and hard.

"I've got it!" Cloe and Moira both dove for it at once, but it was Cloe who hit it with enough strength to send it to Lucinda, who with a strong, single movement, sent it back over the net to Nina's group.

Wham! Here came the ball again, but this time directly at Conner. He followed its path with his dark, alert eyes. It was coming straight for him, he knew. Lucinda yelled something, and Conner stepped back half a step, holding his hands in front of him as Moira had showed him how to do so many times. The ball was coming down now—Conner dropped his hands and swung them back up—his wrists caught the ball at exactly the right spot. But Conner was nervous, and hit it too lightly—the ball flew toward the net, hit it, and dropped down to the ground, rolling a short distance before coming to a stop in a small depression in the ground.

Conner groaned in dismay as Nina's team jumped up and down, cheering themselves hoarse. His face was red, both from embarrassment and from the autumn heat. His pulse was still racing from his bit of action. But worst of all, he'd lost for his sister's team. Anyone else would've been able to hit that, he knew. He'd placed himself perfectly. But he hadn't hit it hard enough—

Moira clapped him on the back. It wasn't a hard clap, but Conner wasn't expecting it, and he stumbled forward, dazed. His twin grabbed his arm, her eyes twinkling in an effort to hide the disappointment in them.

"We'll win next time," she assured him emphatically. "Nina!" she yelled, turning. "Another game?"

"I have to go to work, actually," Nina shook her head. "And Cloe has to come, too. I'll drop her off at home."

Moira shrugged. "Alright, then. Conner?"

Conner bent down, putting his hands on his knees in an effort to regain his strength. He felt drained.

"Yeah, let's go home," he murmured.

Moira inspected his wan face closely, and some of the optimism disappeared from her own. "You okay?"

"Yeah... Yeah," Conner replied, straightening up and pulling his hood back on automatically. His hands, thin and pale, were now sweaty from the exercise.

Moira looked him over again, then turned around to see what everyone else was doing. The victorious team was already leaving; Cloe was going with Nina. Lucinda was waiting for Moira and Conner. The other two girls on their team were already a fair distance away.

"Wanna walk part of the way?" Lucinda asked the twins.

Moira smiled at her. "Sure."

They set off, Moira and Lucinda keeping step in front, with Conner trailing a little behind. The broiling sun looked down on the three as they crossed the court and headed out of the school grounds entirely.

They passed a game of high school football. Conner glanced at the boys almost wistfully. He probably could've signed himself up for the team a few weeks ago, at the beginning of the school year. But experience had taught him only too well the bitter lesson that boys of his lack of strength and weight were entirely Not Wanted in rough-and-tumble games like football.

He hurried his pace, staring at Moira's back while she talked with her best friend. Moira was the older twin by only five minutes. But those five minutes made a world of difference when they were coupled with the popularity, talent, strength, and agility that Moira had and Conner didn't. She was always so mother-ducky, even getting bossy and domineering at times. She totally outshone her younger twin. But, for all that, she never really tried to force him to do anything.

Because it wouldn't have worked. Though the twins didn't have much in common physically, they both had strong wills. And Conner's was actually stronger than Moira's. To those who knew him, it made Conner's physical disability even more of a disappointment. Had he been stronger, he could become great. But it seemed he would always be the frail, passive, pathetic 'runt' he was known as by not-so-sympathetic acquaintances, despite his mother's painstaking attention and diet management. Indeed, it almost seemed that Conner couldn't care less. He did care, nonetheless. But he preferred to keep his one ambition to himself. Shaking off his pensive apathy, Conner suddenly realized that he was falling somewhat behind. He quickened his steps and soon caught up.

"Moira, Mom said we're having a family dinner tomorrow night, right?" he demanded, cutting into the girls' casual conversation.

"Yeah." Moira glanced at him in surprise. "Dad's coming, remember?"

"Oh, that's awesome!" Lucinda reflected. "You don't see him that often, right?"

"No." Conner smiled slightly. "It's been about a month now, so this visit will be special."

"And our cousins are driving down from Pennsylvania," Moira interjected.

Lucinda nodded. "Well, I hope you all have fun. Oh, this is my turn. I'll see you both on Monday!"

"Don't forget about that test!" Moira called after her friend.

four

"It's gonna storm tonight," Moira noted to break the awkward silence between the two siblings, glancing up at the gray skies. "Something like a big storm." Her steps were purposeful. Conner, by dint of hurrying, was only slightly behind.

"Mom said it's going to blow us some cold days," Conner supplied tentatively—and shivered.

"What I like best about cold days is when you go outside and stand in the sun and you're freezing your face off and the sun is nice and warm at the same time," Moira grinned. "You should try it. As in, not wear so much you don't even know the sun is shining."

"But Mom doesn't want me burning myself," Conner muttered feeling his heart rate speed up as he tried to keep even with Moira, who was unconsciously quickening her steps.

"A few minutes won't burn," Moira returned dismissively, with the air of one who'd done it many times.

Conner merely shrugged. "I'll live without it. Besides, there's a heater inside. And a fireplace."

"You should eat more, and the wind won't blow through you like it does. You aren't going to get stronger if you stay inside all day," Moira scolded.

"Just—just leave it," Conner replied, somewhat sharply. The rest of his remark never left the tip of his tongue: *I'm not going to get stronger.*

He and his sister fell silent.

* * *

FOUR

"It's even colder in here than outside!" Conner muttered the next evening, walking into the Italian restaurant with Moira and his parents. He tucked his arms into his sleeves, and shivered.

Moira was already going through the second door and scanning the line waiting to be seated for their relatives. It didn't take her long to find them: Steven and Martha Smyth, and the cousins, eighteen-year-old Percy, fourteen-year-old Mark, and seven-year-old Lila. "Hey, guys!" she called as loudly as she dared in the public building.

It wasn't too long before they were all seated and facing the difficult choice of what to have for dinner. Victoria Whyte, her husband Adrien, and the cousins' parents were soon engaged in pleasant adult talk. Conner glanced over the menu once, then apparently gave up to pull his legs up onto his chair and curl up into a ball to conserve body heat. Percy, after a few minutes of interjecting various comments into the adult conversation, gave up and started doing something with his phone underneath the table. Mark stared at Conner for a bit, then shrugged and watched Percy. And Moira's attention was immediately grabbed by Lila, who wanted to give her older cousin the somewhat tedious history of the princess dress she was wearing.

It didn't take Moira long to grow bored of that, and soon she was wishing Conner would come out of his cocoon and talk to the cousins. Sighing discreetly, she fell into a custom of nodding her head at whatever Lila said and not really replying. She wished she had her phone, but it and Conner's were in their mother's purse, and she didn't feel like bothering her about it.

So she stared at her menu, and suddenly it clicked that she should be thinking about what to order. None of the names popped out at her, so she decided she'd fly by Alfredo like she always did.

Conner was sitting next to her, and she tapped his shoulder with the menu. "Hey," she whispered. "Wake up."

"I'm awake," came a muffled, sleepy voice from the depths of the hoodie.

Moira hit him over the head with the menu this time. "Come on, sit up. You'll get a bad back."

Sighing, Conner lifted his head, keeping his hood on. It was probably a good thing, because his hair was all rumpled and a mess.

Percy slipped his phone into his pants pocket and looked up, much to Mark's disappointment. "Hey, bro, 'sup?" he asked Conner.

"School," Conner returned. "You?"

"College is great," Percy told him. "Are you still at the top of your class?"

"In everything except computer science," Moira answered for her twin, eagerly. "I'm beating him in that."

Percy laughed. "Naturally," he returned. "That's you all over." Moira flushed.

"She had to fix our teacher's computer the other day," Conner put in. "You shouldn't have gotten her that coding book for Christmas. Next thing we know she'll be hacking our school laptops."

"Ha!" Moira laughed scornfully.

"Watch yourself," Percy warned laughingly. "Those things have a self-destruct option, you know."

"They do not," Moira insisted. "Our teacher said they didn't."

"Oh, you asked?" Mark scoffed.

The conversation was interrupted by a waitress walking up to the table. She looked quite Italian, and funny too. Talking quickly and enthusiastically while waving her hands around, she demanded what they all wanted to order.

"*Benvenuto!*" she exclaimed. "So what d'you want to eat, eh?" She flourished her notebook so vehemently that Percy, who was sitting the closest, ducked instinctively. "Past—"

"It's my birthday," Lila interrupted calmly.

"Ohhh, *congratulazioni!*" the waitress breathed, her eyes sparkling with interest. "How old are you, *bella?*" she demanded instantly.

"Seven," the young lady replied gravely.

"How exciting!" Another wide sweep of the notebook. "Anyway, my name's Giulia Pervit—t—to," she finished, racing through the beginning of her sentence and stuttering over the t's in her name, "and I'll be getting you your dinner!"

five

Moira and Conner went with their mother the next day to drop their father off at the airport. Mr. Adrien Whyte worked in a government office in Washington, and he was very rarely home. So they bid him a hearty farewell, expressing sincere hopes that they would see him again soon.

Then came the drive home, marked by silence from Conner, who was carsick, and scattered talking between Moira and her mother. Moira was in the passenger seat, getting a driving lesson. Conner huddled in the middle of the back row of the gray five-seater, keeping his gaze far away from the windows and staring at the floor of the van, with his hands over his ears in a half-hearted, unsuccessful effort to block out their voices.

"There's a train track... Why do train tracks still exist?" Moira asked her mother, leaning forward in her seat. "Aren't they obsolete?"

"Well, people still travel by train," Mrs. Whyte pointed out, keeping her eyes on the road. "And they're good for transporting livestock and other things."

There was a jolt, and Conner bounced up into the air, narrowly missed bumping his head on the top of the car, and landed hard on the seat. He mumbled something and pulled his hood back over his face again.

Moira heard him mumbling, and twisted around in her seat. "Whassup? Need a paper bag?" Her eyes twinkled.

"I will if you don't leave me alone," Conner muttered, glaring at the floor. It was slightly messy, as his mother took it to work every day. There was some mail that had probably been in there for months, as well as a box of tissues.

"I think there's one in the glove compartment," Moira continued, opening it up. "Let me see..."

"M—o—m," Conner protested. "I'm not going to be sick."

"Moira, you'd better leave it alone or you'll spill everything out," Mrs. Whyte advised quickly, glancing at her daughter out of the corner of her eye.

Grinning, Moira pushed the compartment shut and sat back. Relieved, Conner pulled his hood down again and pretended to go to sleep.

"Why are you always wearing a hoodie?" Moira was looking back at him again.

"It's my style," Conner retorted with his eyes shut tight. "Like you with your fingerless gloves."

"Fingerless gloves are cool. Mom, can I have my phone back, please?" Moira asked, suddenly thinking of something she could do to pass the time. They had half an hour left before they reached home.

"It's in my purse," Mrs. Whyte told her. "But you should watch the road so that you'll get more driving experience."

"Alright," Moira conceded.

Conner laughed from the back seat. "Yeah, you'd better be extra careful, because the eldest is more likely to crash than younger siblings," he grinned.

"But I'm not the eld— " Moira began, but something cut her off. Mrs. Whyte tensed, and Conner's face whitened.

"I'm not gonna crash," Moira said finally, her voice much quieter.

* * *

The next day at school, on Monday, everything went well for the twins. There wasn't volleyball that day, so they went home together. Moira went to her room to change, but Conner was still wearing his P.E. clothes because Monday was the boys' P.E. day. In the living room, he took off his hoodie, and pulled his school laptop out of his backpack, working with it on his lap.

He had finished the first math problem when Moira came out of her room, wearing her backpack and holding her phone. Conner looked up.

"Mom texted," his twin reported, reading off her phone. "She's going to work late, so we can either make dinner ourselves or order a pizza." She looked up. "So you pick: pizza, or spaghetti?"

"We went to an Italian restaurant just last night," Conner protested. "Can't we make something else?"

"I guess..." Moira sighed. "What, then?"

"Let's have breakfast for dinner," Conner suggested. "I'll help you make French toast. And we can have scrambled eggs and bacon."

"Sounds great." Moira couldn't help but grin.

* * *

The twins finished their homework, played a board game, and finally got around to making their dinner around five-thirty. Conner felt faint working over the hot stove, and opted to walk to the store and get ice cream for after dinner. Moira approved of that idea, and Conner went to his room to grab his phone.

"I'm going to take the long way," he warned Moira as he stuffed his feet into his sneakers and put them up one at a time on a chair to tie them. "Call me if we need anything else."

"The pantry's stocked," Moira shrugged. "But you could text Mom and ask."

"I'll do that," her brother agreed, tying the last knot. He whistled the first few notes of his favorite patriotic song, *Maryland, My Maryland*, as he stepped out the door onto the front porch, typed a short message to his mother, and marched down the street.

The days were already getting shorter for the winter that would be there within a few months, and a few autumn-colored leaves blew down the street when the wind picked up. The sky was bright and clear, a relief after the giant storm from a few days before. There was the ordinary crowd using the sidewalks—the even more ordinary road traffic.

An old homeless man sat at the edge of the road, waving a sign made from trashed cardboard: *HELP PLEASE.* Conner watched him for a few seconds. He could get something extra at the store with his pocket money for the man, and give it to him on the way back.

With that thought in mind, he waited for the light to change, then crossed the street, making it across just before the light changed again.

He stopped. Someone in the small crowd that was jostling around him had caught his eye.

The man was probably in his mid-forties; tall, stocky, and with a hard, set face. But what really attracted Conner's attention were the clothes he wore. They were of the same hue of the clothes of the bank robbers three years before—and the same style as well, though the man did not wear a mask. Nevertheless, Conner was greatly suspicious. He hadn't seen anyone dressed like that since—

His thin face turned white, and he stared, oblivious of the people around him, his dark eyes following the man to the door of a small gun shop.

Momentarily forgetting about getting ice cream, Conner walked quickly the distance between himself and the gun shop, stopping only at the glass door. There he stopped, and peered in through the glass; he stepped back in surprise. It seemed no one was inside. The lights were off. Conner blinked and looked again. Nothing changed.

But he had seen the man go in there; that, Conner knew for certain. And he saw no other door—remarkably unusual for a store, now that he thought about it. Without stopping to consider, he gently pushed the shop door open. For some reason the bell did not ring. Conner stepped inside the shop, softly guided the door shut, and examined the bell. It should have rung. He had no idea why it hadn't, but he was glad.

six

Conner's spine tingled as he tiptoed around the gun shop, searching for potential hiding places. Making no sound was an easy task for one as light as him. The failing sunlight outside cast eerie shadows in the shop, doubling Conner's sixth sense that something was very off. There was nowhere the man could have disappeared to. And yet—

Walking behind the cashier's desk, Conner saw that the cash register drawer was open. How odd. No shopkeeper with the slightest bit of common sense would leave a cash register drawer open. But now Conner was paying no attention to the money in the drawer; a softly glowing purple button at the back of the drawer had attracted the sixteen-year-old's notice.

With the recklessness of youth, he reached out and pressed the button with one finger, pulling his hand away quickly in case the drawer might explode or something equally drastic. But there was only a slight inrush of air from behind him. He spun around.

A door had slid open in the allegedly seamless wall to reveal steep stairs, going down. The walls of the area were painted a blinding white, and the stairs were made of a shiny, unrusted metal, in a practical design. Conner hesitated only a moment before stepping carefully down the first few steps. He jumped, startled, as the door shut automatically behind him. Frantically he examined it. There was no way out, as far as he could tell.

Conner felt panic welling up inside him as he ran his bony hands all over the door, as high as he could reach, in hopes of finding a sensor that would open the door for him. He found none. The door and the walls were as smooth as paper.

The boy pulled his phone out of his pocket to call for help. He dialed Moira, but the call didn't go through. Then his mother, and the police, with the same result. He tried texting, but his phone was completely offline. Conner felt a sob coming into his throat. He should never have come in here. What was he going to do?

Briefly, he considered pounding on the door and screaming for help, but he changed his mind upon looking down the rest of the stairs. It clearly led to a hallway. And if he'd been led here by that man, obviously someone was at home. Someone who would hear his yelling long before the police did, and someone who could probably very easily dispose of him. Even if Conner *hadn't* been the weakest teenager in Annapolis—whoever had the money to design, or use, a place like this, would definitely be ready for uninvited visitors.

That duly considered, he made up his mind to make the best he could of the situation. Clutching the railing with sweaty hands, he slipped down the stairs as quietly as he was able, afraid that if they creaked someone might come to check. His sneakers made little sound even on the metal of the steps, except once when his shoelaces became so loose that one of them slapped the step with a snap. Conner was horrified; he bent down to remedy the situation. The silence became overwhelmingly oppressive as he sat down to tie his shoes more securely, and sweat broke out on his forehead. His face was already white and pale, and he could feel his heart pounding, so loudly that he felt it must be heard for a mile around.

As he neared the bottom of the steps, he began to hear voices: faint, yet distinct. All his caution, some of which had been dropped along the way, came back to him; he stopped. He had been counting the steps unconsciously; it struck him that there were at least fifty, perhaps a hundred.

Wondering dimly why he felt so fatigued, he gripped the railing as hard as his clammy hands would let him. It seemed that he waited an eternity before the sound of footsteps in the hall died away, and the only sound from below was muffled talking.

Counting to ten under his breath beforehand, Conner descended the last steps and found himself in a hall, as he'd figured he would. Luckily, it was empty. There was an elevator at the far end, and in between about five doors on each side. The doors were unlabeled.

Struck by a sudden idea, Conner took a picture of the hallway, first checking that his phone was completely muted. He put his phone back in his pocket, and tiptoed over to the first door on his right. Softly he put his ear to the door. There were voices within, so he crossed the hall to the door on the left, exactly parallel to the one on the right. All was quiet within but the clicking of a mouse and the quiet clicking of a keyboard. So someone was in there, too.

Conner knew he couldn't stay in the hall, so he quickly checked the rest of the rooms. Finally he found one that he felt sure was empty. He tried the door handle—and it was locked.

Panic again. He started to head for the elevator, then stopped and pulled out his phone. Somehow there was signal *here.*

He couldn't call anyone. He decided to text Moira first. She could get the cops.

His fingers flew across his phone screen as he typed. He stood there, in a corner near the elevator, hoping no one would come into the hall until he got this message across. Even as he started typing he heard the elevator go into motion.

Moira im stuck in a weird place underground and there's no way out that I can find. Plz get the cops. Im in the gun shop by

The elevator doors were sliding open. He had no time left; he had to give the message time to send before he was caught. Conner hit *send,* despite the fact that he wasn't finished, and swiftly leaned the phone on the floor, against the floorboard. He whipped off his hoodie. He could use that.

Someone was coming out of the elevator now. It was the man Conner had followed into the shop, but now carrying a small box. Conner stuck out his foot, and tripped him. The box went flying. Conner immediately leapt on the man, desperate to keep him down on the ground. The man shouted loudly before Conner had a chance to gag him with his hoodie, and he rolled over.

Conner hung on desperately, and somehow managed to continue the roll until he was on top again. He kicked and punched with all his strength, but someone else ran out of the elevator and grabbed Conner's shirt-collar, jerking him off the first man's back, even off Conner's feet. Conner wasn't surprised—he weighed less than a hundred pounds, and even Moira could lift him. Hanging by his shirt-collar did not agree with respiration, however; Conner kicked violently, and grabbed at the hands that were holding him. He could see his phone and the message that appeared underneath his text:

Message could not be sent. Trying again...

Conner abandoned all caution and began yelling at the top of his lungs—yells that got shorter, fainter, and more desperate as time elapsed.

All of a sudden it seemed he was flying—straight at the wall. The next second he blacked out.

seven

By the time twenty minutes had passed, Moira was getting a little anxious. She'd finished preparing the dinner, and was simply waiting for Conner to get back so they could eat. He'd said he'd take the long way, she reflected... But really? This long?

Finally she pulled out her phone. She hadn't gotten any messages, but really Conner should be heading back. She opened it to messages—and froze as a message came in.

Moira im stuck in a weird place underground and there's no way out that I can find. Plz get the cops. Im in the gun shop by

By where? she typed in response.

A few seconds passed, and a thought struck her mind. Immediately, she screenshotted the message and dialed 9-1-1.

Her voice was trembly as she waited for an answer. Moira had never called the cops before. And the message, coupled with the anxiety she'd already felt, made her feel something was dreadfully wrong.

"911, what's your emergency?" came the operator's voice.

Moira forced herself to sound calm.

"It's my brother, he messaged me asking me to call the police. He says he's underground, in a gun shop I guess—"

"Sorry, you're talking way too fast. What?"

Moira bit her lip. Why did the lady have to sound so professionally efficient? It was getting on her nerves!

Slow down, she told herself.

"My brother messaged me; it sounds like he needs help. He said: 'I'm stuck in a weird place underground and there's no way out that I can find. Please get the cops. I'm in the gun shop by—' And there it ends. I asked him where and he still hasn't replied," Moira finished.

"A gun shop? Where is he?"

Moira gave her address, following it with the address of the store she assumed Conner would've gone to. "He was on his way there. I don't know exactly where the gun shop is."

"And you're sure he isn't playing a joke on you?"

Moira flushed.

"Conner doesn't play jokes like this," she insisted.

"His name's Conner?"

"Conner Whyte. I'm his sister Moira. He's sixteen. Mom is at work and Dad's out-of-state." Moira took a deep breath. Her heart rate was dropping back down to normal. Everything would be alright.

"We'll see what we can do," the operator replied after a pause. "Anything else?"

"Can I help you look? I'm at home," Moira requested.

"We'll see," came the answer. The call was ended. Moira wiped the sweat off her face and hit a few buttons on her phone, to see if Conner had sent her anything else but somehow she had missed the notification. There was nothing new—but Conner's text had been deleted.

Moira wanted to scream. What was happening to her twin? She was glad she'd gotten that screenshot. Straightaway she called her mother.

"Moira? Is everything okay? I'm at work, you know," her mother asked, having answered the call.

The words all came out in a rush. "Mom, I've called the police, the message got deleted—"

"Hang on," Mrs. Whyte interrupted. "What's going on?"

"Conner went to the store—" Moira began.

"Yes, I know that; he messaged me. I told him I didn't need anything. And?"

"He messaged me asking me to call the police. He said he was underground and in a gun shop, or something like that. I don't think he was able to finish the message. I called the police and they said they'd look into it. And now the message has been deleted—but I have a screenshot," Moira finished.

Silence for a moment.

"What are the police doing?" Mrs. Whyte demanded. Moira detected something odd in her voice, even over the phone.

"They said they'll check up on it. Can I ride with them, Mom?" Moira asked eagerly.

"They're there? At the house?" Her mother's voice was sharp.

"No—no, not yet. Can I go and help look for Conner?" Moira requested again.

"Wait—I'm going to come home. If they get there before I do, ask them where they're headed, and wait at home for me. We'll follow," Mrs. Whyte decided. "Meanwhile, don't bother your dad. He doesn't need to worry yet."

"Okay. Okay." Moira nodded emphatically, though her mother wasn't there to see it.

"And you? Are you okay? Did you guys eat dinner yet?" Mrs. Whyte could sense the fear and stress in her daughter's voice.

"Yeah, I'm fine. No, we didn't eat dinner yet. It's ready, though," Moira added quickly.

"Well, you eat something, and I'll see you soon. I'm going to let my boss know what's going on, and I'll be home in fifteen minutes. Eat something, okay?"

"Okay," Moira forced out. "Goodbye, Mom."

"'Bye," Mrs. Whyte replied. She hung up and grabbed her purse.

At the house, Moira forced herself to obey her mother and force down some of the dinner she and her brother had made. The minutes—even the seconds—dragged by until she saw the car drive up the sloped driveway to the Whytes' home. Moira flew out of her seat to the door, running out onto the driveway even before her mother had gotten out of the car.

"Mom!" she yelled, the moment the car door swung open.

"Whoa!" her mother exclaimed, getting out and getting nearly knocked over. "You're a nervous wreck!"

"Look," Moira held up her phone. "That's what he said. Can we leave right now? And look for him?" she pleaded.

Mrs. Whyte read, and re-read, the message. Only her trembling hands revealed the emotion behind her well-controlled face.

"Any sign of the police?" she asked quietly.

"No, not here," Moira returned.

Mrs. Whyte's indecision lasted only a moment.

"Get in the car. We'll look, ourselves."

eight

"How on earth did he get in here?"

The man whom Conner had attacked was brushing nonexistent dust off his clothes, having picked himself up off the floor. He spoke with a harsh and jarring voice. His hair was dark, contrasting deeply with his light blue eyes.

His companion, who had thrown Conner against the wall, was a yet more muscular man, dressed in much the same style of clothes. He glanced derisively at the boy before looking much more respectfully at the man who was obviously his leader.

"No idea. But there is only one way from the outside into this sector, no?" he asked.

Slowly, the other nodded. "Yes, yes. Run a security check. But how is the kid?"

"The kid?" his henchman echoed. He used his foot to roll Conner over onto his side. "He's alive—he was getting help!" he exclaimed, reaching down for Conner's phone. The other watched him pensively as he inspected it, and deleted the message, which had finally been sent. "He never finished it. But someone read it," he surmised finally. "I will alert security, in case there is an inspection of the shop." He pushed back his sleeve to reveal a sort of band on his arm that had a smartphone on it, and hit a few buttons.

"Wait, Maughan," the other interrupted him suddenly, staring at Conner. "This kid comes at a most opportune time. Tell Dr. Lafferty that he need not postpone Test T4 after all. We have a testee."

"You want to test on *him*, Dr. Arnnu?" Hilton Maughan asked in a low voice.

"He's not—"

"Children should learn not to go snooping around," Lyndon B. Arnnu broke in. "They're as bad as cops, some of them. Take this one to the lab. And you have five minutes to find out and report to me how he got in here, and five more to fix it before the cops get here—if they do."

* * *

"So, there are only two gun shops within a reasonable walking distance of that store. This one is closer to the house location, so we're headed here first." One hand was taken off the driving wheel to point to a built-in car GPS. "This shouldn't take long."

Two policemen were in the car, one driving and the other in the passenger seat. In the back sat a large, full-grown German Shepherd. The policeman in the passenger seat looked annoyed.

"I wouldn't be surprised if it was just a prank call," he muttered. "Kids these days never think."

"The operator told me the girl on the phone sounded terrified. I don't think it's a prank," the other replied.

He was a well-built man of perhaps thirty years, tall and muscular. He wore a police badge and a plain uniform. His light hair was combed neatly back, and clipped onto his belt was a practical handgun. The name on his badge read *Darek Lasek.*

A few minutes later, he parked the police car on the side of the road, bringing it to a neat stop with the wheels exactly parallel to the curb. He and his companion hopped out, the dog following them.

"Rocky," Darek spoke softly, and the German Shepherd bounded to his side.

Ignoring some curious looks from street pedestrians, the two policemen narrowed the distance between themselves and the glass door of the gun shop, and strode in. The bell above the door tinkled as Darek opened it and ordered Rocky to remain outside. The two policemen headed into the shop.

It was relatively small, with only a few racks. The cashier, sitting at a desk near the back, looked up as they entered. He stiffened.

"Good day," Darek greeted him, smiling. "We're just here to check up on a story of a kid that's stuck in a gun shop. Seen anyone?"

"Nah," the man replied, shaking his head. "Business is really bad today."

Darek and his friend walked around the gun shop briefly. Nothing looked suspicious.

"Alright," Darek decided finally. "We'll go look somewhere else. Have a good day." That said, they walked out, where Rocky was waiting with the patient air of a well-trained dog.

"Hey, boy," Darek greeted him. The three got back into the police car and started for their next destination.

"I told you it was a prank," Darek's friend scowled.

Darek pushed his foot down harder on the pedal. "We don't know for sure yet."

* * *

"There they are," Moira pointed eagerly over the dashboard at the cops' car, driving away from the gun shop. "And there's the gun shop." She unbuckled herself.

"Hey, wait until I've parked," her mother cautioned her, bringing the car to a stop not half as precise as Darek's had been. Moira was out of the car and sprinting for the gun shop in an instant.

"Moira—wait!" Victoria shouted after her. Moira was already going through the door. Sighing worriedly, Victoria rushed after her, stopping barely a moment to lock the car after them.

Moira burst into the gun shop, looking around as if she expected to see Conner right away. Her face fell after the first few seconds.

"Conner!" she yelled.

The salesman behind the counter was already staring, and now he left his place, as Victoria grabbed her daughter's hand. "Conner?" the man questioned. "My name's Hilton Maughan. There is no Conner here."

"He's my brother, where is h—" Moira began, her eyes sparking dangerously.

"Moira," her mother cautioned, watching Hilton's face change from polite to angry.

"You mean the kid the cops were looking for?" Hilton demanded. "They already left. They didn't find him. He's not here."

"He said underground," Moira spoke up—and immediately set to jumping hard on the floor. "Conner!" she yelled again. Where on earth was he?

"Stop that!" Hilton roared. "If you're going to damage my shop, I will call the police!"

"Moira!" Victoria exclaimed. "Mr. Maughan—you're sure he isn't here?"

"I already said no," Hilton retorted rudely. Moira scowled.

"Moira, let's go," Victoria decided. She wanted to find Conner just as badly as Moira did, but she had to look out for Moira as well. "He's not here. Let's look somewhere else," she forced herself to say. Gently but firmly, Victoria took Moira's hand and led her from the shop.

"Kids really are worse than cops," Hilton muttered to himself.

nine

Hours later, they were home again, after a fruitless search throughout the entire city. Victoria told Moira to get a drink and go to bed. Completely unable to sleep, Moira listened as her mother phoned the police and then Mr. Whyte.

"No, we haven't found him... Since around six this afternoon. Yes, it's been five hours at least... I sent Moira to bed. She's terribly high-strung. I think she's asleep, thankfully..." Victoria was saying.

I'm not, Moira thought to herself, listening with all her might.

"I don't know yet whether or not to send Moira to school tomorrow. If she goes she'll have to take the bus—I don't want her walking around in the streets without Conner... No, don't fly down here yet, especially if you're busy. I'll call you tomorrow and let you know if anything's turned up. If not, maybe you wanna come, I don't know..."

Moira bit her lip. She didn't want to go to school without her twin. Not only would he be missing and she be worrying about him all day, but she'd be asked questions all day—a type of popularity that Moira absolutely hated.

"Right. Goodnight. Love you, dear." There was a soft sound as Victoria put her phone down on the kitchen table. Then a creak as she sat down in a chair.

Moira pulled the covers over her head, tossing and turning alternately for about five long minutes, her mind filled with thoughts of her twin. It was only a long time later that she managed to fall asleep.

* * *

"It was a terrific success. He's completely ready. Congratulations on your victory, Dr. Arnnu."

That was the first thing he heard. The voice was faraway and distant, but he sensed that the faintness was in his own ears. There was beeping. Slowly the sounds straightened themselves out. He sat still. Something was wrong. He had no idea who he was, where he was, or what was going on. He remembered nothing. His breath started to come faster.

"Perfect. Now let's have a look at our young friend, shall we?" This voice was hard and unemotional.

Footsteps approached the chair. Pushing down the panic, he opened his eyes to a world he had never seen before.

It was obviously a laboratory. At the far end of the room were some computers; one of them displayed a heart rate. Then there was a table, and it and everything on it was covered with a white sheet. On another, smaller table, was a metal box. There were some things like metal wardrobes against the walls. Three doctors were in the room, one at the computers, one writing something on a clipboard—and the last, staring at him out of light-blue eyes. By the door stood six security, dressed from head to toe in hard metal or plastic or something else—he couldn't tell.

The doctors were all dressed uniformly, with dark gray pants and a laboratory coat. The first two doctors wore medical masks and gloves, but the one who was looking at him did not. He was tall, with dark hair.

Now, he looked down at himself. He was strapped in some sort of chair, dressed in the same sort of material that the doctors wore: dark gray tunic, with elbow-length sleeves, and pants. It struck him that what he could see of himself looked extremely muscular and well-built.

He glanced up at the doctor, who was still watching him. He wanted to ask the question most prominent in his mind, which was filled with swirling thoughts, all of them screaming at him to fill the blank. But something was wrong with his self-control; he felt strangely half-asleep.

"Good morning, Trooper. How do you feel?" he was asked. Though busy with the rush of disintegrating questions, his mind processed an answer immediately. He felt limitless, ready to run a marathon, capable of anything.

Unconsciously his hands curled into fists—strong fists, that looked as if they had the potential to wreck metal. The only exception was his vague, indecisive mentality. He felt somehow powerless to process. But he could answer the question.

"Okay," he said. His own voice, hesitant and boyish, sounded strange in his ears. "I feel okay."

A smile from the doctor. "That's good. Do you remember anything?"

"Do I remember anything?" he repeated dazedly. "No. I don't. Who am I?" he managed to make himself ask.

"You, my friend, are Trooper A1," he was told. "I am Dr. Arnnu. You are the first to be successfully given the T4 injection. Congratulations on becoming the first 'superhuman'." The doctor's smile widened. "Unfortunately, I don't think your recollections of the past have stayed with you."

"Superhuman?" Trooper echoed. Lyndon nodded.

Instinctively, as if to test his supposed strength, Trooper tested the firmness of the bonds that held him to the chair. He felt as if he could break through them easily. But Lyndon's voice interrupted. "Don't mess around with that."

Trooper relaxed his arms, with a dull sense of surprise at his own cooperation. Gradually it came over him that he—his mind—wasn't really in control. It was the doctor's commands.

Now Lyndon ignored him, walking over to the table with the small box. He pulled it around so that Trooper wouldn't be able to see the contents, and put his finger down on a portion of the lid. It sprung open.

Trooper sat still in his passive position, seemingly ignored by Lyndon and the others. He had very little scope for movement with the straps located periodically along his arms and legs, and it struck him that it would be nice to get up and stretch his legs. He felt incredibly bored, with blood surging through his veins, and yet he sitting there lethargically. And the bands would be so easy to break, he could tell. But somehow Lyndon's order weighed him down.

He sat there, moving nothing but his eyes. A clock on the wall read seven in the morning, and he watched the minutes hand move across half an hour's distance. During that time he grew continually more restless, the urge to break free and find out exactly what was going on, growing. But it was only an urge. Somehow he was unable to act on it.

By the end of that time, the two unintroduced doctors had finished whatever they were doing, and one of them walked over to the chair Trooper was in. Trooper followed him with his eyes, as far as he could, until the doctor went behind his chair and hit a button. Something beeped for a moment.

"One hundred ninety pounds," the doctor remarked, the satisfaction plain in his voice. "Very good."

"How much before, Dr. Lafferty?" Lyndon asked, looking up from his box. "Half as much, correct?"

"Yes." Dr. Viator Lafferty came around from behind the chair, and Trooper could see him nod. "Half as much, about."

"Excellent." Lyndon stepped over to the chair, holding some kind of purple band in his right hand. With his left, he hit something on the side of the right armrest, and the straps on it retracted into the chair. Trooper's right arm was free.

"Lift it," Lyndon ordered. Trooper obeyed mechanically, and Lyndon fit the band around his wrist. There was a soft click as something locked. "You can put your hand down now," Lyndon told him. Trooper did.

Lyndon looked over him for a moment before nodding his head and hitting a few more buttons. All of the straps were retracted.

"Stand," came the command, followed by the unanimated compliance. Trooper looked down from a height of about six feet. There was a dim awareness that he had never been this tall before...or maybe, he realized, it was just that he didn't remember. Standing up gave him a strange, yet supreme, sensation of strength. His legs felt like new, though they wanted to be stretched. And to do that stretching, he had an odd feeling that he could run a marathon.

His hair was in his eyes; he pushed it back with one sturdy, broad hand. He noticed that it was a light blond, and it went just past his ears—longer than any of the doctors'. He wondered if that had anything to do with the T4, whatever that was supposed to be.

"You see?" Lyndon asked him, watching his face closely. "You do what I tell you. Dr. Pizzey?"

The doctor by the computers turned around. He was short, with a worn and wrinkled face that spoke at least forty years. "You, Trooper," he addressed him. His voice seemed tired. "Jump."

Immediate submission. Lyndon's face broke into a giant smile, and he burst into laughter. The other doctors smiled as well.

"Now," he said when he could speak, "we have won. Trooper. Trooper A1." He pointed to the six security standing by the door. "Teague, Medole?"

Two stepped forward. "Doctor?"

"Fight," Lyndon ordered, stepping away from the three.

ten

She's a girl, dressed all in black, riding a black motorcycle down an empty street. The wind rushes by the helmet covering her head and blows about the little bit of her brunette hair that sticks out. She feels free, and pushes the motorcycle to its greatest speed. There's a pothole in the road. For an instant, she is flying... The wheels hit the ground again, and bounce a couple more times before staying on the ground.

She sees someone in the distance. It's a young man, dressed in a purplish soldier's uniform. She gradually brings her motorcycle to a stop, coming to a standstill just a few feet away from the man. He looks up. It's her brother.

"Hey, Conner," Moira greets him. Somehow he looks healthier and stronger than he's ever been in his life. And taller. Moira slams the kickstand back, and hops off her motorcycle, running to her twin. She stops upon seeing the look on his face. Robotic. Impassive.

"Conner!" The shout re-echoes, again and again. It turns into the sound of a siren, repeating and gaining in volume. Moira puts her hands over her ears.

* * *

Moira sat bolt upright, the scenes of her dream flashing through her mind. Suddenly she realized that the "sirens" were her 7:30 alarm for school. Automatically she threw her hand out, hitting the *Snooze* button instead of the *Alarm Off* by mistake. She never got up right away at 7:30.

"I need to get a motorcycle," she muttered, and dropped back on her pillow—then the events of the day before flooded into her head. She sat up again, leaping out of bed.

That was the first morning since the first day of school that she finished her morning routine within five minutes. As she went out of her room into the hall, brushing her hair quickly, she saw that her mother was already up, and on the phone. Holding her finger over her mouth as she listened, Victoria pointed toward the kitchen. Moira nodded, mouthed a *Good morning*, and tiptoed down the hall to the kitchen, finding a plate of buttered toast on the table. She hadn't eaten much the night before, and it took only the sight of the toast to make her ravenously hungry. She was just finishing the third slice of the three when her mother came into the room. Quickly she finished.

"Moira. Good morning," her mother addressed her. Her face was lined with wrinkles. Moira could tell that her mother hadn't slept much the night before.

The daughter felt guilty. As soon as she'd fallen asleep she'd slept like a log until her alarm went off. Only six hours at most, but she still felt refreshed.

"Any word of Conner?" she asked swiftly, though the answer was already on Victoria's face.

Victoria shook her head. "No. They want us to wait till six PM before calling him in as a missing person. So I expect we'll just have to wait. Your father is flying in tomorrow, or the soonest he can get a ticket on such short notice," she added as an afterthought.

"Okay. Okay," Moira repeated herself. "Can we go looking again?"

"No, we've done all we can," Victoria told her. "I have work today, and you're going to school. Did you finish your homework?"

"Yeah." Moira nodded. "We both did."

"Good," Victoria approved. "Now, finish your breakfast and get ready to go, or you'll be late for the bus."

"Can't I walk?" Moira pleaded.

A quick shake of Victoria's head. "No—Conner isn't here to walk with you."

"But—" Moira began, then broke off. It made no sense, seeing that she was so much stronger than her brother. But their parents had always been strong advocates of the buddy system.

Within ten minutes, she found herself running for the bus stop; she had about two minutes before the bus would arrive. Her hair, blowing in her face, reminded her of her dream, and she looked about in vain for Conner. But of course there was no sign of him.

A couple of students at the school she went to were already at the bench where they ordinarily waited for the bus. They were both in grades lower than hers; she didn't know their names. They looked up as she approached, and she waved distractedly. The school bus was coming down the road now, slowly. Moira ran harder and made it on the bus after the other two did.

She grabbed a handhold and looked around as the driver told her to sit down quickly. Moira listened for a moment, and heard her friend Cloe's voice; she followed it to a seat near the back of the bus. But Cloe was sitting with her brother Jack.

"Hey, Moira," Cloe greeted her friend, surprised. "Whassup?"

"I need a—" Moira's voice broke off as the bus jolted into motion and she grabbed the back of a seat just in time.

"Jack, move," Cloe hissed at her older brother. He got up, keeping a hold on the back of the seat, and moved carefully into the aisle, glancing at Moira's worried face momentarily. Relieved and grateful, Moira sank into the seat next to her friend.

All around them was the chatter of students from ages six to eighteen, but that didn't daunt Cloe in the least, and she was extremely curious as to why Moira was taking the bus to school, alone—and without her backpack. Ignoring Cloe's agonized glances, Moira stared at the back of the seat in front of them vacantly.

Finally Cloe decided that sighing loudly and looking anxious wasn't getting her anywhere. "Psst. Moira. What's wrong? Where's Conner? Where's your backpack?"

Moira jumped. "My backpack? Oh, no, no," she moaned, patting the front of her white blouse for backpack straps, and finding none. "I must've left it at home. I'm dead."

Cloe giggled. "Nah, we can sit together. But where's Conner?"

"Yeah, where's Conner?" Jack echoed. He'd taken the seat behind the two.

"Wimpy Conner," someone nearby in the bus added maliciously, snickering.

"He's playing sick, isn't he?"

Moira tensed, but Jack recognized the bully's voice and issued quiet threat for that person to hold their tongue or deal with the wimpy Conner's stronger friend.

"Conner disappeared," Moira told her friend, sitting back and closing her eyes. "Since yesterday."

A startled gasp. "You're kidding!"

"No," Moira shook her head briefly. She realized her shoelaces were coming untied after her run for the bus, and was glad of the excuse to look down and tie them.

"What do you mean, 'missing'?" Jack asked from behind.

"He's just gone." Moira decided not to complicate matters by talking about the gun shop, etc. "Mom's gonna call him in as a missing person later."

"Why not now?" someone asked.

"Because he hasn't been missing for twenty-four hours yet," Cloe retorted, as if the answer was obvious.

"Hey, how long does this thing take to get to school?" Moira asked quietly, as the bus slowed to a stop for some other kids at another part of the city suburbs.

"Probably twenty minutes now," Cloe told her, checking her watch. "We'll get there five minutes early. You can run to the principal's office and explain about Conner and your backpack."

"Hey," Jack interrupted from behind them, "do you guys have any suspicion of what happened to Conner?"

"Yeah," Moira muttered. "He disappeared."

"Yeah, but when, why, and how?" Jack persisted.

"Do I look like a detective?" Moira returned stonily. The others took the hint, and left her alone.

eleven

It was then that Trooper discovered that if his decision-making and thinking was slow and foggy, his ability to obey was not impaired in the least.

The instant after his mind processed the cool command, he turned to face his two opponents, and sized them up. Both were slightly shorter than him, and had the advantage of the protection that their suits afforded them. Trooper, on the other hand, had no protection at all except for the tunic he wore.

Nevertheless, the command had been given, and Trooper's mental state left him with no choice but immediate obedience. Therefore he charged.

The other two had obviously been expecting the match, and had their own orders, for they made no effort to retrieve the rifles they carried on their backs, but instead waited for Trooper with trained serenity. Unperturbed, Trooper slammed his fist into the first of them. The fight had begun.

* * *

Three hours later, Trooper had reached the point of intense physical exhaustion. Lyndon had had him fighting nonstop, against ever-increasing numbers. Trooper seemed to have had no training at all, but he pulverized six, held his own against fifteen, and was now gradually losing to about twenty. His breath came in great, drawn-out gasps as he continued to throw punches and dodge blows; still they came on and on. Then came relief, in the form of a shout that Trooper barely heard over the pounding in his ears.

"Stop!" It was Lyndon's voice. The soldiers stepped back, leaving Trooper to lean against the wall he had gotten against his back, and pant for breath. Bruises were forming all over him. He felt like collapsing.

Lyndon walked over to him, looking him over. He nodded, and smiled. "Good. Excellent. Those will heal," he added, noting Trooper's puzzled expression. His face fell. "You really disappoint me. No militant schooling at all. But what else to expect from a sixteen-year-old?"

That answered one of the questions still racing through Trooper's mind, or the part of it that wasn't in control. So, he was sixteen, was he?

He locked eyes with Lyndon, desperate to speak of his own accord. He just couldn't understand why not. But somehow it felt physically impossible. He—the real he—was caged.

Lyndon ignored the eye contact, staring back for a moment before looking away. "Dr. Lafferty, can you take Trooper A1 to his new quarters? And, Dr. Pizzey, start the process of collecting an army, will you?" He smiled. "Two hundred security are not enough to take over an entire nation."

* * *

A few minutes later, Trooper found himself alone in a tiny, bare room with a rude cot and a closet. He turned as the door clicked shut behind him—there was no knob on the inside. There was nothing more to see, and he was still exhausted, so he collapsed on the cot, falling asleep almost instantly.

* * *

He is outside, wearing a uniform like those of the security he was fighting earlier. From neck to foot, over his other clothes, it is a seamless suit, plated with some kind of hard material, yet the inside is as pliant and supple as a diver's suit. Overall the thing is surprisingly light. His head is protected by a helmet made of the same hard, exterior substance; but the inside is cushioned. Over his eyes is a dark eyeshade, tinted so that what he sees is various shades of purple. He looks up at the sun and notices that the visor deflects the sun's from his eyes completely, so that he can actually see the sun. It is white, with just the slightest tinge of purple.

When he looks down again, his neck aching slightly, the setting has changed. He is still outside, but on the roof of some high building. It looks like a school building, at least six stories high. There is a scraping sound, loud in his sharp ears as amplified by the helmet. He wheels around.

A girl of about sixteen is standing on the roof. Her shoulder-length, light-colored hair waves about wildly in the wind that seems to be trying to blow her away. But she keeps her balance on the flat roof, staring away from him. She is wearing what is obviously a school outfit: blouse, skirt, tights—and sneakers.

Trooper hears a loud voice suddenly, coming through a communications system on his helmet. "Clear the roof." It is Lyndon's voice.

Trooper glances down at the gun in his hand, then back at the girl. She obviously has no idea he is there. Every instinct of the captive Trooper revolts against the order. But the robot Trooper knows only to obey.

Mechanically he cocks the rifle. It is already loaded. Slowly Trooper lifts it, taking perfect aim.

For a moment it almost seems that he is regaining control over himself. His hand wavers, and sweat breaks out on his forehead. But inexorably his fingers tighten.

Suddenly the girl turns around, and her dark, deep eyes widen in shock. Her mouth opens in a silent scream that the wind carries away before Trooper can hear it. But suddenly Trooper realizes he knows this person. He doesn't know her name, and he doesn't know why he knows her—but he knows her.

And then somehow he is in control. He relentlessly forces himself to ignore the radio command and lower his weapon. But there is a sharp pain in his right wrist, and the gun falls from his grasp. The sting goes away, but his hand feels paralyzed...

* * *

Trooper sprang up on the cot, his breath coming quick and fast. For the first time in his memory, he felt awake. He looked around the small room, new panic rising to the surface. His eyes darted from the knob-less door back to the clothes he was wearing, and vivid in his imagination was the image of the girl he had seen. He had seen her before. He knew that.

There was another sting. He glanced at his right wrist, and saw the strap Lyndon had put there earlier in the long, weary day. His only guess was that it was injecting something into him and that accelerated the sixteen-year-old's fright. But even as he flipped his hand over to see if he could find a way to get it off, he lost control. He closed his eyes and tried hard to remember his dream which seemed to have linked him to his forgotten past.

But it was already fading away.

***

That day began a new life for Trooper—new in the truest sense of the word. Every morning was an automated injection. Every day was training. And every night was either experimentation or sleep.

As the days went by, he stopped dreaming. The unknown past was nonexistent. There was only the present. The scared, confused sixteen-year-old dissolved into the tall, silent, powerful, and dangerous machine, willing and eager to carry out his superiors' every command.

But that was just the beginning.

twelve

No school day had ever passed so slowly for Moira. It seemed that every moment she was waiting for her mother to call her cellphone, even though she knew full well that she would never do such a thing during the school day. All during the long, tiresome classes, she fretted. Someone came in late to school; Moira imagined for a moment that it might be Conner. By the time the day was over, she felt like a nervous wreck.

But nothing happened all day, from the moment she woke up to when she hopped on the school bus to go home. She was quiet for the ride, in a seat in the back by herself, and no one bothered her. Victoria wasn't home when Moira arrived, and so the girl raced through her homework, finishing it an hour later.

It was four-thirty when she pushed her laptop shut and stuffed it into her backpack, along with her math book. She sighed, and sat back on the couch.

Brushing her hair out of her face, Moira found herself trying to think like a detective. What could have happened to Conner?

He could have been kidnapped, of course. That would explain why his message had been cut off. But what would kidnapping have to do with a gun shop and underground? In fact, why had Conner been in a gun shop at all? He was on his way to get groceries, not to buy guns.

Another long, drawn-out sigh. Moira drummed her fingers on the couch cushion. Suddenly her phone started ringing.

Snatching it up, Moira glanced at the name only half a second before hitting *Accept Call.* It was her father.

"Hello, Dad," she breathed, suddenly aware that her voice was all trembly.

"Hey, Moira. Any news on Conner?"

How on earth could he sound so calm? Maybe it was an adult thing, Moira decided.

"No," she told him quickly. "Not that I know, at least."

There was a short pause.

"Well, then," Adrien said finally. "You okay?"

"Yeah," Moira replied softly.

"Mom's at work? Are you home alone?"

"Yeah," Moira repeated.

"Well, take care of yourself, okay?" Her father's voice was quiet and gentle.

"Okay." Moira nodded, even though he couldn't see her over the phone. With her free hand she brushed her long bangs out of her eyes. "Okay. See you. Love you, Dad." She said it naturally, after long years of her dad working far away from home.

"Love you, Moira. 'Bye."

There was the dial tone, and Moira dropped her phone on the sofa.

Would it never be six o'clock?

* * *

The lecture hall was giant, but was only one of the many at this college. It was after school hours, so the seats were only half filled. Near the front of the room, the professor went through a demonstration of nuclear physics on the board. Most of the students in the room weren't really paying attention, as attendance at this lecture was only for those who wanted to do better in class.

"Come on, we went over this last week." The teacher tapped the board with her pointer, making a few of the students jump and look up guiltily. "You have got to know this. Trinity Ryder?"

A tall, slim eighteen-year-old young woman stood up from her desk. Her shoulder-length hair, a dark brown, was dyed light purple at the tips, including her long bangs that hung over her face. She wore boots and a short skirt. The collar of her purple jacket, which matched her eyes, was unfolded in a revolutionary style twist.

"Fission means splitting up. Fusion means combining." Her voice was level, casual, and had a Californian accent.

"Very good," the teacher approved as Trinity slipped back into her seat. "Everyone else, you have simply got to memorize that. Now..."

Trinity's phone vibrated in her pocket, and she pulled it out, holding it underneath her desk.

Everything's ready for you to come home, Vi. When can we expect you?

Trinity sighed softly, and typed a quick answer.

Next weekend. See you soon, Dad.

She turned her phone off, and looked back up at the teacher and the board, but with new meaning in her unique purple eyes. Idly she tapped her desk, as if impatient for the lecture to end.

* * *

It startled Moira the next morning when her morning alarm went off and her phone started ringing at the same time. She hit the alarm off and answered the phone.

"Moira." It was her mother. "Are you awake?"

"Yeah," Moira mumbled, pushing the hair out of her eyes.

"You're going to have to handle breakfast on your own and take the bus. The police called; they want me at the station. I'm sitting outside there now, in the car; I was just waiting for your alarm to go off before I called. Got that?"

Moira jumped up in bed. The police station?

"Why? Did they find something about Conner?" she demanded, throwing off the sleepiness that hung over her.

"I think they did, but they wouldn't tell me over the phone." Victoria paused. "I'll let you know as soon as I find out, whether you're in school or not, okay? Now you'd better get ready for school."

Moira cringed and shut her eyes. If the police hadn't wanted to communicate the news over the phone, it must be something bad...

"Okay. I'll see you soon, Mom," she forced herself to say.

"Goodbye, Moira."

Moira dropped her phone on her bed and hopped down to get dressed.

thirteen

It didn't take nearly as long as Moira had worried. Within a few minutes of her boarding the bus, her phone started to vibrate in her pocket. Ignoring the curious looks of Lucinda, with whom she was sitting this fine morning, she answered it immediately.

"Moira, can you talk?"

"Yeah, I'm on the bus. Are you done there?" Moira asked eagerly.

"Yeah." A long pause. "Do you want the good or bad news first?"

"The good news, please," Moira breathed, her voice choking. What had happened to her twin?

"Well, we won't know anything for sure for a few days."

That's not helpful, Moira reflected morbidly.

"What's the bad news?" she made herself ask, shutting her eyes tightly.

"Okay, well...They might've found out where Conner disappeared to. They found some clothes on the banks of the harbor in an out-of-the-way area... And Conner's wallet and phone. And there was... There was blood on the clothes."

Moira caught her breath. A chill went down her spine. For a moment she was frozen, unable to speak.

"I—is it Conner's?" she whispered.

"That's why they had me come to the office. They took a sample of mine. In a few days we'll know," Victoria finished. "That's all. Are you okay? Do you want me to pick you up from school?"

"N...no, I'll be okay," Moira assured her, dazed.

"Good. There you go. If you need anything, call me. Dad'll be here tonight—

we'll both drive to the airport to pick him up. Sound good?"

***

Later that day, she didn't know whether to be glad or regretful that she'd stayed at school. It had given her an opportunity to mask her feelings completely before returning home. But half the time she'd been there she'd felt she was stuck in a horrible nightmare, and the other half she'd wanted to run throughout Annapolis till she found her brother. She had paid no attention at all, and it was a good thing for her that her teachers had some sense of what was going on and didn't call on her.

Victoria picked her up after school. Moira noted the bandage on her mother's arm with something like silent horror.

"How was school?" Victoria asked after the first few minutes of driving were passed in complete silence.

"I dunno," Moira mumbled. She opened her mouth to speak a couple of times before the words actually came.

"Did...did they show you Conner's stuff?"

"Yes, it was all his. They said they can give it to us when they don't need it anymore for their investigation," Victoria explained.

Moira shuddered. "What was it like?"

Victoria set her lips together tightly, and avoided the question by skipping ahead on the conversation topic. "Their theory is that someone attacked him on the harbor and...threw his body into the water," she finished, her voice wavering curiously. "I told them it makes no sense, seeing as he was nowhere near the waterfront, and Conner was on pretty good terms with everyone we know. But the things are undoubtedly his."

"Mom, what are we gonna do?" Moira whispered, biting her lip. She shut her eyes tight and tried to drive away the image her imagination conjured up, an image of her twin— No. She wasn't going to think about that.

"What do you mean?" Victoria forced out, playing for time. But Moira could see her face in the rearview mirror, and Victoria's face was white.

"Wh—what if they can't find Conner?" Moira asked.

"Moira, really. Change the topic." Her mother's voice was dangerously edgy.

Moira stared out the car window miserably.

Conner, where are you?

* * *

Giulia Pervitto, the Italian waitress the Whytes and Smyths had met at the restaurant on Saturday, was not accustomed to seeing unsavory-looking customers in the highly rated restaurant. In fact she noticed that the manager gave them glances as if he was considering kicking the two out, especially when they didn't wait in line to be seated but claimed a lone table on their own. But the manager seemed to be a peace-loving man, and when he saw that the intruders weren't causing any difficulties he decided to merely let them be.

However, Giulia was relatively young. She'd been hired primarily for her bouncy, cheerful Italian heritage, and not for her lack of curiosity—which did not exist. Though it must be said for her that when she was sent to get some glasses from the cupboard nearby that table, she had the sincere intention of going straight there and back without any lingering. But the words "superhuman army" caught her, hook, line, and sinker.

The next string of words, whispered in deep masculine tones, nearly made her drop the glasses. "When does the war start?"

"Encephalon says about two months," came the quiet reply. "Are you in?"

"Sure." A coarse laugh. "Where? When?"

"Here, in a week. Upstairs. They'll ask if you want to see the cook, and you have to say you want to speak to the manager instead. Spread the word. Just to our type, of course." Here there was a soft chuckle.

Giulia caught her breath. This—this was—

"What's the gain?"

"The gain? You kidding me, man? You've got life long super strength to gain, and loads of spoils. Global!"

Giulia didn't wait to hear any more. Clutching the glasses tightly, she turned and fled.

Dropping off the glasses at the kitchen counter, she made her way to the ladies' restroom, pulled out her phone, and dialed 9-1-1.

fourteen

Having called the cops and given them a rundown of what she'd overheard, Giulia made her way back into the main partition of the restaurant, glancing over at the table in the corner. Her face fell. The two men were gone.

Giulia's eyes flew across the restaurant. Had someone warned the plotters that she was calling the police?

But it was too late to retract the call now, and so Giulia forced herself to return to the kitchen while keeping her ears open and eyes peeled for signs of the police. And tried to ignore the sinking feeling that they'd call the whole thing a prank.

It didn't take too long, as it was only a few minutes before she heard sirens and saw red-and-blue lights flashing at the windows. The car came to a stop directly outside the restaurant. Customers stared, and one of the waiters ran for the manager, who was upstairs. Giulia merely watched out of the corner of her eye as she stirred a pot of spaghetti vigorously. She smiled slightly as she realized that she was the one and only person who knew why the police were here and who had called them. It was a strange feeling.

And she had never called the police before.

The manager of the restaurant, a short, stocky Italian, made his grand entrance just when the police, two of them, walked in through the fancy front doors. But he didn't seem to notice the police at first, but only the black-and-brown dog which trotted in energetically before them. His face grew dark.

"No dogs in here!" he hissed at the hapless employees who happened to be within hissing range. Including Giulia. "Whose dog is this? Get it outta here!"

"Hey, sir, it's mine," one of the policemen broke in. "Rocky—out," Darek Lasek added calmly, making a quick gesture to the dog.

The manager tensed visibly when he saw the policemen, and immediately became docile and more polite. "Hello, what brings you here?" he asked in his thick Italian accent.

"Someone made a call," Darek told him quietly. "Some customers here are talking about an army and a war?"

"Customers?" A vehement hand gesture. "Nah. I have good customers here!" the manager added proudly.

"They left," Giulia ventured, popping out of the kitchen and wiping her hands on her apron.

All eyes swerved to her. "What?"

"They were sitting there," the Italian twenty-two-year-old answered, pointing to the table. "I overheard part of the conversation, and called you. When I got back out here they were gone." She shrugged.

"Well, there isn't much we can do about it," Darek pointed out dryly. "Do you have a description?"

"Yeah." Giulia looked around at everyone in the crowded restaurant. "You want it—here?"

"No, no." Darek shook his head. He looked at the manager. "Sir, do you have a back room somewhere where we can discuss this?"

"Sure," the man nodded. "Come right this way."

* * *

"Sorry for the trouble, sir," Darek told the manager a few minutes later as they went back into the main partition of the restaurant. He touched the brim of his police force cap lightly and turned to leave. Giulia had briefed the officers on everything, and they'd even collected fingerprints. If either of the two patrons were on the criminal record, they police would find out who they were.

There was a moment of silence after the door closed, while the other restaurant customers stared for a bit and went back to their meals. The silence didn't last long, however. The manager was furious, though he had managed to hide it while the police were there.

"You called them!" he spluttered at Giulia. "Do you want to ruin my business!"

Giulia dropped her gaze to the floor. This was bad.

Who had warned the men?

"No!" she replied, her voice raising automatically. "But if you hear people talking—talking terrorism—you call the police!"

"You were spying on my customers?" The manager's voice rose to its highest pitch, making him sound almost hysterical. "My restaurant will never live this down! I don't care what they were talking about—you can talk to me first—and obviously you're making things up! Miss Pervit—t—to," he mimicked her stutter mockingly, "you're f— "

Giulia flared up instantly. "No, I quit!" she yelled before he could finish the sentence. "And I quit *now!*" she finished, waving her arms furiously.

There was more stunned silence from everyone else around, but the manager didn't lose a beat. "Then get out now!" he roared, without flinching.

"I am!" came the angry retort. Giulia tore off the restaurant-logo apron, tossed it onto one of the empty tables, and flounced out.

* * *

That evening, Wednesday night, when Moira and Victoria came home with Adrien from the airport, the two parents went up to their room to talk. Moira was left alone downstairs.

She had no appetite for homework, and threw herself on the sofa, wondering whether to cry or go to sleep. Homework was horrible. Falling asleep would be horrible. She wanted to cry, but she couldn't. Everything was all so unreal and horrible.

It reminded her of when Ricky had died, three years before.

She and Conner had been thirteen. Adrien worked in Washington back then, too. Conner and Ricky had elected to go on a walk, and Victoria and Moira had stayed home to make dinner together. That had been fun—until the phone rang with the crushing, devastating news. The weeks after that were all blurry. Life had been shattered. But somehow, little by little, the Whytes had learned how to live again. Conner's traumatic nightmares had gotten fewer and fewer. They had sewn their lives back together and become a normal family again.

And now Conner, too? Moira wanted to wail. It wasn't fair. It couldn't be real. Conner had to be fine. He was just stuck somewhere. He wasn't dead.

No way. He wasn't. He couldn't be. It was impossible. She couldn't live without her twin!

She bit her lip so hard she could taste blood, and stared at the ceiling, trying to slow the avalanche of panicked thoughts. Then she looked down.

On the coffee table in front of her was the newspaper Conner had been reading last Thursday. Almost a week ago. Distracted, she picked it up and flipped through the pages.

The untimely death of some famous actor was bewailed by the headlines. There followed a few pages of various reports, including one on global warming, another on some interesting specimens of food poisoning, and more. Moira merely scanned them all until she came to the report on the bank robbery.

She had read it on Thursday. Now she read it again and tried to follow the thought process Conner might have taken. Being his twin, it wasn't all that hard.

He must have decided to keep his eyes out for the color he had seen the gangsters wearing. Maybe he'd seen it, and that led him to the gun shop.

And there something had happened. How he'd gotten from the gun shop to the waterfront she had no idea, but that's how it appeared. And from what she'd gathered from her mother, the police were of the mind that someone had killed him there and thrown the body into the river. No one would find it.

She suddenly realized with a burst of shock that the message to her could have been typed by someone else. The police had found other fingerprints on the phone—

But no, she dismissed that thought almost immediately. The phrasing, punctuated by periods—that was intrinsically Conner. She could tell. As well as the meticulously careful spelling.

So the message was from him. Of that she was certain.

Moira read the description again, and this time the urge to investigate herself was stronger. A wave of recklessness passed over her.

"Tall, dark gray clothes. I can manage that," she breathed aloud, and suddenly paused, drawing her breath in swiftly as she remembered a conversation she had had before.

She and Conner. Two months after the first bank robbery. They'd decided to find the robbers. The decision had only lasted two hours of running around Annapolis together and pointing out to each other people wearing dark clothes. There had been a brief bit of excitement when they'd found someone who was wearing a mask as well—but it had been some kid who was playing a game with his sisters. That was Jack. His family had just moved to Annapolis, and that encounter had knit the beginnings of a close relationship between their families. Because Nina had quickly detected that the twins were lost, and she, Jack, and Cloe had walked home with them.

But Conner had been careful to let Moira know exactly what color they were looking for. They had phones then, and he'd found what he decided was the closest thing to it on a color selector.

"But that's in the purple range," Moira had objected.

Conner had shrugged. "That's the closest I can get," he'd told her. "And now that I think about it, there was the slightest hint of purple. Or violet. I dunno."

So it was purple they were looking for.

Or violet, the memory reminded her. Her jaw was hard and set.

fifteen

Victoria came down a few minutes later, having washed her face carefully and pasted on a smile, in hopes that it would make Moira feel better. Adrien was on the phone with the police—some officer by the name of Darek Lasek. Apparently he was handling their case.

Reminding herself to keep smiling, and to give Moira whatever hope she could, she stepped into the living room. Her brow furrowed. Moira wasn't there.

But a piece of paper was on the couch. Swiftly Victoria crossed the room and read the message.

Hey Mom, I'm looking for Conner. I'll be okay. See you soon. Love, Moira.

Victoria gave a strangled, horrified gasp, and fished her phone out of her pocket. It took her only a moment to hit her daughter's contact.

The phone was ringing. For thirty-one seconds Victoria waited breathlessly for an answer. The voicemail!

Victoria nearly had a heart attack. Why wasn't Moira answering? She dialed again, but there was no answer this time, either.

Staring at her phone a moment in disbelief, Victoria ran upstairs. "Adrien! *Adrien!*"

* * *

Almost half an hour later, Moira stopped, leaning against a street lamp post to catch her breath. She'd been running. Looking for Conner. And for people dressed in purple—or violet. But half an hour of running had put an end to that. Moira was exhausted, and she hadn't seen anyone. But common sense was starting to break in now, and telling her that this was crazy, that she wouldn't achieve anything. Not by running through the streets at night. But really, Moira couldn't care less.

After the primary wave of weakness had passed, and she'd regained some strength, she pulled her phone out of her pocket. She was rather surprised that she hadn't heard anything from her parents in all this time. But her surprise vanished instantly as she saw the first notification.

21 missed calls from "Mom."

"Oh, joy," she muttered, realizing that her phone had been muted the entire time. She was dead. Totally dead. Just dead.

Heaving a long, despondent sigh, she braced herself to return the call.

Her mother answered the instant it rang. "Moira! Moira?" Her voice was frantic.

"This is me," Moira replied weakly. "Sorry, Mom, my phone was muted and I—"

"Moira, I called you twenty times!"

"Twenty-one," Moira whispered, cringing.

"I'm not even going to start discussing how much trouble you're in over the phone. Your father's been cruising, looking for you. Where are you?" Victoria demanded.

"I...I don't know," Moira mumbled, turning on her phone's flashlight and looking around for a street sign.

"Moira—!" Her mother was almost screaming.

"Crossing between Conduit and Union," Moira shouted.

"Conduit and Union. Right in the middle of the city!" her mother groaned. "Now, you stay right there, and if you've moved an inch by the time your father gets there, I'm going to—!"

* * *

"I don't suppose I have to explain to you that your mother is extremely angry, eh?" Adrien remarked quietly as Moira got into the car. Her clothes were soaked; it had started to rain. She looked utterly miserable. And Adrien had a tired expression on his face.

"I was looking for Conner," Moira presented by way of explanation, dropping herself wearily into the passenger seat.

Her father's face seemed to become only more tired. "The police will find him if anyone can," he pointed out. "Are you going to close the car door?" he added, glancing her way and noting the dripping clothes and the disheveled hair to which the water had given a black hue. It clung around her face, making her look miserable.

Moira pulled the door shut mechanically, having to open it again and slam it so that it actually closed. The car lights turned off, but regardless of the dark, Adrien didn't miss the fact that Moira tried to brush her hair back with her hands. She discovered a leaf that had got in it somehow, and pulled it away, and stared at it pensively.

"There's another one there," Adrien commented, glancing at his daughter one last time before he took his foot off the brake and coasted down the slight incline of the street.

Moira brushed her hand over her hair till she found the second leaf, and pulled it off, dropping both of them onto her lap. "I think there must have been leaves in the gutter," she remarked ruefully.

"You didn't have to stay right there, you know," Adrien stated. "Why'd you take your mother literally?"

Moira shrugged. "I didn't really want to move," she had to admit. "I was wondering where Conner could be. I don't think he's dead, Dad. He's got to be alive somewhere."

"We didn't want to believe that Richard was dead, either," Adrien reminded her.

"No, but we didn't have a choice," Moira pointed out. "We had no choice but to believe. But I really think Conner's alive," she repeated earnestly. "I'm going to find him."

"You can't go disappearing on us like that," Adrien told her mildly, turning off the high-beam headlights to allow another car to pass them. Moira didn't really answer him.

"What if we were to lose you, too, Moira?" Adrien asked her.

The sixteen-year-old didn't answer that, either. She just stared out the window at the dark street, eventually starting to shiver in her drenched clothes.

"Moira," her dad finished finally, "we may just have to accept that he's gone."

"He isn't gone," Moira broke in. "I know he's alive, D—"

"Moira."

And the rest of the ride was quiet.

sixteen

Friday afternoon was when Adrien got a call asking him to drive down to the police station. Moira and Victoria were home, so they went along as well. It wasn't good news, Moira could tell in the air. No one spoke a word the entire drive. When they arrived, Moira dashed out of the car and up the single step, beating her parents into the front room of the police station. They arrived soon enough, though, and identified themselves to the officer behind the desk.

"Mr. and Mrs. Adrien Whyte," Adrien told the officer. "And our daughter."

"Whyte," the officer nodded, though the glance he cast at Moira was not exactly a welcoming one. "We've been expecting you. Step this way, please, will you?" He pointed them to a door. "Third door on the left."

"Thanks," Adrien nodded, leading the way.

The room was small. At one side, there was a desk, where a female officer was sitting. There was a table, and on it were Conner's jacket, wallet, and phone. The jacket with some traces of red on it. Moira flinched visibly.

The officer stood up from her desk as they entered the room, and turned around to face them. Her face was friendly, but she wasn't smiling.

"Mr. Adrien Whyte, Mrs. Victoria Whyte, and Miss Moira Whyte?" she asked.

"Yes," Adrien answered for them all.

"Niamh French. Nice to meet you. Now, I have some things to tell you. Mrs. Whyte, the results came back. They matched," Niamh told the mother, the police officer's voice and manner businesslike.

"So it's Conner's?" Victoria asked quietly.

Niamh nodded, her eyes downcast. "Secondly, we found several different sets of fingerprints on the articles over there." She pointed distractedly to the things on the table. "Most of them weren't in our records, but one set was. They belong to a former drug dealer by the name of Reginald Tauber who was released from jail two months ago. Officer Darek Lasek is handling your case, and he's out looking for the perp right now."

"A drug dealer?" Moira echoed before she could restrain herself. "Why? Conner was nowhere near the waterfront...?"

"It appears that he was," Niamh shook her head. "I'm sorry for your loss," she added, glancing up at the parents. "I really am. We'll update you once we find out more. We're done with the articles; you can take them with you when you go. Any questions?"

Looking dazed, Adrien shook his head, but Moira answered before either of her parents could. "Were you able to track where he went, using the phone?" she asked. There was something in her voice that made Victoria look at her. Something fierce, something almost calmly despairing.

Niamh stared at her. "Yeah, actually, there was an embedded tracker that isn't usually found in that phone model. Do you know anything about that?"

"Yeah," Moira nodded. "I put it there," she admitted slowly.

"Well, you did a good job." Niamh smiled slightly. "It was pretty well done for an amateur."

"Thanks." Moira's white cheeks flushed slightly, and Adrien squeezed her hand.

"Would you like to see his route?" Niamh continued, gesturing toward her computer.

Moira shook her head. "N—no thanks," she managed to stammer.

Niamh looked slightly startled, but she shrugged. "Mr. and Mrs. Whyte, do you have any questions?"

"No." Adrien stepped forward, picked up Conner's jacket, and wrapped the wallet and phone in it. He tucked them underneath his elbow mechanically.

"Sorry—one more," Moira whispered, biting her lip.

Niamh nodded. "Yes?"

"May I please have your phone number?"

* * *

Darek and four other police officers were on their way to Reginald's place at that very moment, in two police cars. One officer rode with Darek and Rocky; the others were in the other car. It didn't take them long to reach the waterfront, and only a couple more minutes to find the place they'd been directed to. But the moment Darek, who'd been driving the leading car, pulled up in front of the house and got out of the car, they saw a figure running away from the back of the run-down house.

"Stop!" Darek yelled, but to no avail, as the man sprinted for the street. With lightning speed, Darek threw himself back into his seat and started the engine of his patrol car.

"Don't get out!" he yelled to the other officer, who had his door open and his seat belt unbuckled. The next instant they were on the chase. Looking slightly dazed, Darek's companion just managed to slam his door shut and started buckling his belt.

"The target's getting into a car!" Darek yelled into his microphone to the other patrol car.

"We're following you," came the reply.

Darek stared ahead at the target's car beginning to move, slowly at first but picking up speed. The policeman put his foot down on the pedal. The murderer wasn't going to get away!

From the fact that this part of the waterfront was a favorite criminal resort, Darek knew the street layout pretty well. And so even as the chase began, he was thinking of a way to cut the criminal's car off. He put his plan into action by yelling into his microphone again.

"Pete! Keep chasing him. I'm going to block him after three intersections. Keep me posted!"

"Righto!"

Slowing the car so he could turn down a side street, Darek glanced momentarily at his companion. "Got your seat belt on?"

"Yeah," the other replied. "Why?"

"This is gonna be a wild ride." Darek suited action to the words by pressing hard down on the accelerator.

The tires squealed horribly as he turned another corner, and now they were running a route parallel to Tauber's. "One!" Darek called out to himself, swinging the wheel just in time to avoid slamming into the back of a truck. They passed a crossing, and Darek caught a glimpse of the pursued car.

Obviously they were going the same speed.

"Two!" he yelled, accelerating the car even more. His companion braced himself for the turn he knew was coming. Rocky howled.

"Lasek! They're coming on third!" a voice shouted through their earphones.

"So are we!" Darek exclaimed, jerking the steering wheel to the left sharply. There was another loud skidding sound that could be heard even above the sirens.

Their car was racing directly into the path of that of the criminal. Darek slammed on the brakes, intending to block the road with his car. Reginald Tauber would have to stop his own car, and the other patrol car would come up behind him. The criminal would be cornered.

But things didn't quite go as expected, and Reginald had been driving too fast to stop in time. He screamed as the cops' car shot into the road ahead of him and his own car rammed into theirs.

seventeen

SMASH! Shattered glass spewed everywhere. The policeman in the passenger seat shouted loudly as he flew forward into the dashboard—a shout completely drowned out by Darek's piercing yell and Rocky's accompanying howl.

The yell was Darek's first reaction. His second reaction was to look down at himself.

Reginald's car had slammed directly into his door at an angle, catching Darek's left hand between itself and the dashboard of Darek's car. The hood of Reginald's car had pushed its way through the door all the way to Darek's chest, which he now realized hurt horribly. But even worse was his hand. It hurt—like—

He could dimly hear the police from the other car jumping out and running to the scene of the crash. His companion was totally out.

The arrest was being made, and the other officers were pushing Reginald's car away to free Darek. A moment later Darek's left hand fell down to his lap. It had been crushed by the twisted metal, and was bleeding hard.

"Officer!" one of his compatriots exclaimed. "Can you get out of there?"

"No," Darek gritted. He tried moving even just his hand, and was met with a spasm of pain that made him gasp for breath and would've made him double over if it hadn't been for his screaming ribs.

The policeman stuck his head into the car. "Hold still. The ambulance is on the way."

"Rocky—"

"He's fine. Relax."

Darek shut his eyes. There was so much pain. He knew instinctively that his career was totaled.

* * *

The first thing Moira did upon arriving at home after a long drive of absolute silence was follow her father and mother into the house. But she didn't appear to be brokenly dazed as did her parents. She closed the door behind them and caught her father's arm. He turned to look at her. She saw something in his eyes, something deep and sad, and hesitated a moment before making her request in a voice curiously strong.

"Dad, may I have Conner's phone? Please?"

* * *

That afternoon was bright and sunny, but the sun's cheerful, golden beams found it unexpectedly hard to pierce their way through the dark blue curtains of Moira's bedroom. After repeated tries, they seemed to give up. Barely any light at all shone through.

Moira was inside, sitting at her desk, busy at work on her father's old computer that he let the twins use sometimes when they needed a computer. Conner's phone was plugged into it, and was sitting besides the old-fashioned computer box, its screen showing a strange display for a smartphone. Clearly, Moira was busy at work, hacking it. A terminal was open on her screen, and she was typing in various command lines, pausing often to consult a *Hacker's Guide* lying open on her desk. Its pages were held open to a section on *Tracking* by a mug of iced tea; Moira was being exceedingly careful not to upset it. It might be added here that she considered something to drink an essential for productive coding, almost as necessary as the Guide. And a cup of iced tea, or even better, a mug of hot chocolate, could last her for hours when she was really absorbed in her work.

It didn't look as if she'd be disturbed anytime soon, either. The door was locked, and her parents weren't going to start banging on it for a while yet.

It was suppertime, but no one in the Whyte home had any appetite. So Moira jumped when her phone started ringing, and looked up almost guiltily before realizing it was her phone and not something—or someone—else. Whipping off her headphones, through which she'd been listening to an inspirational soundtrack, she picked it up off the floor where it was plugged in, and answered it. It was her best friend Lucinda.

"Hello?"

"Hello, Moira. Oh my. I'm so sorry. I heard the news!" Lucinda burst out. "Is it okay that I called? Are you okay? What are your parents doing?"

Moira wondered how Lucinda knew. Probably Victoria had told Lucinda's mother, who had told Lucinda.

"Yeah, I'm okay," she replied, acutely aware that it probably wasn't an appropriate time to admit to anyone that she'd gotten over her initial shock and now was absolutely determined to find Conner. A determination that allowed for no lingering sorrow. She knew he was alive, somewhere, probably needing her help. But other people just couldn't understand the instinct that connected the twins.

"That's good. And your parents?" Lucinda asked, pulling her phone away from her face momentarily so Moira wouldn't hear her sigh of relief. She'd been afraid Moira wouldn't be in the mood to answer the phone.

"I think they're gonna be okay. They're all cut up like they were...three years ago, but I think they'll recover," Moira finished.

"That's good." Lucinda's laugh was nervous and strained. "What are you doing today? Are you gonna be at school on Monday?"

Moira glanced back at her computer, and frowned. "Umm... I dunno. I hope not."

"Well, what'll you be doing?" Lucinda pressed.

"I'm...working on something," Moira explained vaguely.

"Okay, well, I'll leave you to it." Lucinda decided. "I hope you guys are okay. I'll see you soon, Moira, sound good?"

"Yeah." Moira smiled faintly. "See you soon."

eighteen

No sooner had her friend hung up and Moira taken a sip of iced tea than Moira's phone rang again. Hurriedly she put her cup down and picked it up.

"Hello?"

"Hey Moira, it's Cloe. Any news of Conner?"

"Uhh—"

"Nina just got home from work. She told us that today she had to help get a policeman to the hospital. He crushed his hand in a car accident and broke a couple of ribs. She says he's off the force for good!"

"Ouch!" Moira exclaimed, wondering what connection this bit of news had with her twin.

"But she heard about what they were working on. Apparently a Conner Whyte got murdered? *Not* your brother, right?"

Moira licked her lips. "Umm... Actually..."

"You're joking?" Cloe's voice lost all its excitement. "C'mon Moira—"

"It's Conner, unless there's some crazy coincidence," Moira broke in. "But Cloe, I don't think he's dead, 'kay? Who was the police officer?"

"Darek Lasek," Cloe told her quickly. "Darek Lasek, and Nina thinks his hand's gonna be paralyzed for life! He's gonna be in the newspapers!"

Moira cringed. But thoughts of her brother were prevalent in her mind at the moment, and though she did feel sorry for the policeman, she turned her attention to other matters almost right away.

"Cloe? You still there?"

"Yeah," came the quick reply.

Moira glanced at Conner's phone, then at her screen, and chewed at her lip thoughtfully. "Can you go on a walk in half an hour? And maybe Nina and Jack? I'll meet you at your place. I'll ask Lucinda, too."

"Your parents are gonna let you go walking after what happened to Conner?" Cloe demanded incredulously.

Moira gave a short laugh. "Maybe if you guys are with me."

"Okay. I'll ask my mom and text you."

"Sounds good. See ya!" Moira hung up, pulled her chair in, and set to work feverishly. Five minutes later she sprang out of her chair, grabbed both her phone and Conner's, and glanced around for a jacket.

Her favorite pink hoodie wasn't on the back of her chair like it always was. She gawked for a moment before realizing it must've gone into the wash. Moira knew very well that she had other jackets in her closet, but suddenly a thought struck her, and she started rummaging around for something dark.

Not finding anything, she finally gave up on a jacket altogether and went to ask her parents for permission to go walking with her friends. It'd been a few days since her "adventure," so they let her go, with the stipulation that she'd stay with her friends the entire time and keep her phone unmuted. As Moira left the kitchen, she spotted Conner's dark blue coat-jacket hanging on the rack by the door. He wore it almost everywhere, but apparently he hadn't been wearing it that fateful evening.

She picked it up off the hook, and, after a moment of hesitation, shrugged her arms into its sleeves. It fit her perfectly.

Her mother watched her go down the street from the kitchen window. Adrien was sitting at the kitchen table, stirring a cup of coffee that had long gotten cold.

"Do you think she's trying to ignore it?" Victoria asked softly. "She seems to have recovered already. She looks...almost normal."

Adrien frowned down at his coffee. "I can't tell."

* * *

Twenty minutes later found Moira at the Marwicks' front door. Cloe, Nina, and their brother Jack were there waiting.

"It's a great day for a walk," Cloe commented.

Jack just glanced at Moira. "Isn't that Conner's?" he asked quietly.

"Yeah. I'm sure he'll want it back...when we find him," Moira told them cheerfully, jogging off in the direction of Lucinda's house. The three Marwicks followed.

"Didn't they find proof that he was murdered?" Nina broke in, glancing hard at Moira.

Moira stuck her nose in the air defiantly. "I won't believe it until I see it!"

* * *

"It's really good to see you like this," Lucinda told Moira upon stepping out her front door. "I was afraid you'd be all cut up and depressed. But look at you—you're actually smiling!"

"I don't think Conner's dead," Moira told her straight off, as Lucinda fell in line. The Whyte girl was leading them all, her feet taking her quickly where she wanted to be.

"Really?" Lucinda pressed.

"Yeah," Moira told them seriously. "*We* all know that there are things science can't explain! Like God and creation and—"

"And the bond between twins," Cloe finished for her.

"Where are we going?" Jack wanted to know.

"We're going to form a detective club," Moira announced, without really answering the question. "Lucinda, you're in charge. I'm the hacker. Nina's the medic. Jack's the manpower. Cloe's the notetaker. Sound good?"

"Whoa, whoa, it's your brother we're looking for," Lucinda broke in. "You be in charge, Moira. I'll be... I'll be the secretary."

"Okay, I guess," Moira grinned. "Sure."

"What's it called?" Jack drawled.

"I dunno," Moira shrugged. "Any ideas?"

"Antikillers," Cloe said almost immediately.

"You mean antkillers?" Jack scoffed.

"N—o!"

"Whyte Detectives," Lucinda interjected.

"Are you racist?" Jack demanded, turning a chuckle into a cough. Nina swatted his shoulder as a warning to behave.

"No, no, we're not racist," Lucinda amended hastily.

They'd reached a small gun shop. Now Moira stopped, and everyone else followed suit. "Here we are," Moira announced quietly. "Everyone ready?"

"What are we gonna do?" Cloe asked eagerly. She was the youngest in the gathering of five.

"Jack, Cloe, and Lucinda, can you just distract the shop owner?" Moira requested in reply. "Nina... I might need your help."

With that, and after pulling the hood of Conner's favorite coat low down over her face, she pushed the shop door open. The bell above the door tinkled merrily.

* * *

"I knew it," Moira breathed a few minutes later. "I knew it." She stared at her phone screen.

"What?" Nina whispered, bending over her shoulder. They were blocked from the shop owner's view by a rack of guns.

Moira turned off her phone screen and stood up. "There's a firewall here," she told Nina softly. "Redirecting the GPS signal, and I don't know what else—yet." She pursed her lips, and signaled to Jack, Cloe, and Lucinda, who were talking loudly nearby. "I'll get through that wall and find out what these people's game is. For Conner's sake, I mean it."

"How long will it take?" Nina murmured in her ear as the five walked out of the shop together.

Moira allowed a pent-up sigh to escape her. "Could be a day, could be months. Only time will tell."

nineteen

The gun shop bell rang again only a few minutes after Moira and her friends left. This time, the newcomer was strikingly different.

She was tall, with beautiful, deep violet-colored eyes. Her long dark brown hair, dyed a light purple at the tips, cascaded loosely down her back. She wore high-heeled boots, a slick, dark purple overcoat, and a multilayered skirt in various shades of pink and purple. But she walked with the graceful air of a lady conqueror.

She walked straight up to the front desk, her silver-and-sapphire earrings tinkling slightly as she looked down. "I want an AK47, a stunner, and a VK02. If you get 'em to me in thirty-two seconds then I might let you get me some more."

Hilton smiled and stood up. "Why do you bother with the password? Your dad's been waiting all day. Come on back, Lady Violet." He pulled out the cash register drawer, and didn't lose any time in pushing the button at the back of it.

"It's Trin," Trinity Ryder returned as the secret door slid open silently. "Or Ryder."

***

"Vi!" Lyndon Arnnu exclaimed as Trinity and Hilton walked into his office downstairs. Hilton remained standing deferentially by the door with two other security guards. Trinity Ryder, also known as Violet Arnnu, ran forward to hug her father.

She was taller than him by only a few inches, and he looked up at her, his eyes full of fond pride. "It's good to see you again, Vi."

"You, too, Dad," Trinity whispered, dropping her cool, imperious airs for a moment. Her purple eyes sparkled happily.

A moment later, and the father recovered his dignity. "Well, Vi—Trin, you know why you're here."

"You've finished," Trinity supplied, most of her smile disappearing.

Lyndon nodded happily. "Yes. The guard has all had it; their new name is Inters. Would you like to see?"

Trinity merely shrugged. "Sure."

Lyndon glanced beyond her. "Trooper, step over here a moment, will you?"

One of the guards by the door, a tall, muscular young man with the build of a strong adult but the facial expression of a teenager walked over slowly. Trinity glanced at him momentarily.

His longish hair was a light blond, and his dark eyes were piercingly haunting. He was dressed in a combative-style uniform: purple helmet with visor, purple jacket, purple pants and boots. He wore elbow-pads and knee-pads that were of a different tint, but nevertheless of purple. Bristling with arms, he made a formidable picture.

What was it that really attracted her attention? Maybe it was the dead look in his dark eyes. Or the way he passively obeyed Lyndon's command, as if he were a robot. In fact Trinity wondered for a moment if he could be human.

"Who is that? I haven't seen him before," Trinity told her father slowly, looking over at him.

Lyndon shrugged. "He was snooping around one day and so we decided to test on him. It just happened to be the day we discovered what worked. So here we have a random kid off the streets, the first supersoldier. Trooper A1."

Trinity opened her mouth to say something, but Lyndon didn't notice, and continued: "He was a wimpy kid. And look at him now! We wiped his memory, and we've got him on a sedative, since we have no idea where he's from. We still tested his loyalty, of course; he obeys every command without compunction, and instantly. My men have been putting him through vigorous training, as well as going through it themselves. The army will be ready in a couple of months, just as soon as we've drafted whom we choose from the criminal status. The tryouts begin next Wednesday, city wide."

"Sedative?" Trinity smiled slightly. "Is it the water compound? It seems to work like a charm," she added.

"It is," Lyndon nodded. "Of course, the Annapolis population won't have as concentrated a dose as Trooper here, but I daresay they'll be generally passive enough to listen to orders. Obviously we're going to have people who don't drink city-sourced water, but their number will be insignificant, and they won't be able to group together effectively. The Dendrites and Sensors will help us mark them for observation," he explained. "And, of course, you'll be in charge of Annapolis, and later Maryland, from the start. I need to go straight to Washington once we get started here. You can handle things?"

Trinity laughed. "Are you kidding, Dad? You've brought me up to take charge of the world—literally."

Lyndon smiled and patted her shoulder affectionately. "Good. Follow me and I'll show you the revised battle plan."

twenty

Giulia Pervitto hadn't forgotten about the restaurant episode by the time Wednesday came around. She puzzled over it the entire morning, and finally resolved to show up at the tryout at the restaurant that day. She'd see if she could get any information for the police.

That decided, around four in the afternoon, she dressed in dark, unobtrusive clothes, muted her phone and dropped it into her pocket with a gun, and set off.

Upon arriving at the restaurant, she walked in right away, after parking her car a safe distance away and starting her phone recording sound. The restaurant looked quite ordinary, but she knew what she was looking for, and didn't miss the fact that there was a waiter just standing near the stairs at the back of the restaurant. He was facing the wall, obviously using a phone with low brightness on. Discreetly she made her way over to the stairs, blending in with the general flow. But as she lifted her foot to mount the first step, she saw the waiter approach her, and paused.

"Are you here to see the cook?" he whispered.

Giulia was already tense, but this if anything confirmed her suspicions. Something was definitely going on here.

"No, I want to speak to the manager instead," she replied, wondering if the password-taker could hear her pulse racing.

He didn't seem to. "Go on up," he directed. "First door on the right."

Giulia went up the stairs alone, feeling the suspense terribly as the sounds from the main restaurant grew fainter as she went on.

She had never been up here before, and now she noticed that the stairs opened out into a dark hall with black carpet on the floor, walls, and ceiling. The only light was afforded by a single row of faintly-glowing bulbs along the center of the ceiling.

She could hear muffled talking from inside the first room on the right. Quietly, her face drawn and pale, she laid her hand on the doorknob. It turned easily, and a moment later she was in.

This room was more brightly lighted, though the black carpet continued even here, producing a gloomy atmosphere. There were two lines of people, one male, one female. With only some slight hesitation, Giulia joined the female line, all the while looking about curiously. People gave their names to dark-clothed officials. On either side of the door stood a sentinel, dressed in a dark uniform, heavily armed. The only sound in the room was the quiet murmur of voices.

Only too soon, even before she really got a grip on herself, her turn came. The questioner asked her name.

"Giulia Pervit—t—to," she rattled it off, trying to keep herself calm and composed.

"Martial experience?"

"Uhh, none at all," Giulia returned, slightly startled at the question.

The interrogator looked at her closely out of hard, suspicious eyes. "Area of expertise?"

"Just cooking," Giulia replied, trying to laugh although she was sweating and internally freaking out.

Another callous, scrutinizing look. "I don't believe you belong here?" the interrogator asked, raising his voice.

All other activity in the room froze. Giulia felt all eyes turn to her.

"Where's Pizzey?" the interrogator asked, looking around at everyone else. Giulia swallowed hard.

"In his office," one of the guards by the door replied. "Sir!"

Looking at him, Giulia formed the estimate that he was just a typical soldier, though somehow he appeared abnormally strong. So did the other.

But there was something about the tall, light-blond-haired man with the boy's face that told her she'd seen him before. She couldn't quite put her finger on it. But she knew she'd seen him.

"Go get him," the interrogator instructed. "And be quick." Saluting—a strange salute, where he touched his left shoulder with his left hand—the soldier left the room, shutting the door behind him. The interrogator smiled politely at everyone who was left in the room.

"Please be patient for a few minutes," he told them quietly. "We'll resume as soon as this is taken care of." But he was still watching Giulia, very closely.

It didn't take Brooks Pizzey long to arrive on the scene, and when he did, Giulia was startled. He was, apparently, the restaurant manager! She jumped back, staring. He stared in turn.

"Giulia Pervitto," he identified, without having to check the record. His face broke into a slow smile. "I had a feeling we'd be seeing you around again."

Giulia stuck her hand in her pocket, feeling for her phone. She was moderately confident she could figure out how to dial the police without looking. And it was better than the alternative.

Her fingers brushed her gun and closed around it. That might prove even more effective than a phone call at the moment.

"Unfortunately, you've seen and heard too much," Brooks continued. He turned to the guards. "Trooper—liquidate."

The robot soldier came suddenly to life, looking straight at Giulia. "Sir!" he nodded, acknowledging the command.

In the split second that followed while Trooper pulled his rifle off his shoulder, the crowd in the room melted to the sides, leaving him a clear range to fire. Giulia pulled her hand out of her pocket, with her loaded gun in it; thinking fast, she shot up at the ceiling, shattering the single, powerful bulb.

The room was instantly dark, save for the few sparks that the torn cords produced. A few people screamed. Brooks roared in fury.

"Trooper, get her! And Staunton, stay out of it. This is his!"

Trooper tapped a button on the side of his helmet. Powerful light purple lights lit up along the top of his visor, cutting an arc of eerie violet light across the room. Holding his rifle at the ready, he looked around for Giulia—and saw her at the other side of the room, punching the screen out of the window she'd already opened. She grabbed the windowsill and swung herself out, dropping down to the pavement below.

"Now, Trooper!" Brooks yelled.

Giulia rolled off a van directly underneath the window, landed on the ground, and twisted her ankle, but she picked herself up immediately and limped down the street as best as she could manage, zigzagging between the pedestrians.

Trooper ran over to the window, firing his rifle after her. Every shot missed, and the target disappeared around a corner. Trooper put his free hand on the windowsill, ready to leap out, but an order from Brooks stopped him.

"Stop! Not in that uniform!" They couldn't afford to expose themselves yet!

Trooper paused, and backed away from the window. He hesitated, looking at Brooks.

"Staunton, get after her now, but first go get undercover. She needs to be eliminated, and soon." The other guard nodded, jerking a black, hooded poncho out of his pack and pulling it on. "Trooper, your aim is an unacceptable. I'll get to you later on it. Everyone, we have to evacuate now. Don't come here again until Pervitto is liquidated. You all have my contact information. Now, scram!"

twenty-one

"It's pathetic," Trinity remarked to her father, watching the whole scene on a computer. "Correction: *he's* pathetic. Do you really still think your sedative is worth the time? On him, at least?"

"What's wrong?" Lyndon asked her. He stood behind her chair, looking over her shoulder.

Trinity scowled at the screen. "The whole way he goes about things. That's not professional."

Lyndon shrugged mildly. "He's a kid, remember—"

"How young?" Trinity cut in.

"At least a full two years younger than you," Lyndon replied. "He can't be older than seventeen."

"So why do you keep him at all?" Trinity asked, looking annoyed. "I could fight better than that with one hand tied behind my back."

"Since we've taken the trouble to equip and train him, we may as well keep him around," Lyndon explained. "He's somewhat expendable and will follow orders."

"Drugged like that, he's useless," Trinity retorted firmly. "He has no value on his own, and his aim is pathetic," she continued savagely. "He's horrifically slow and has no idea what to do during combat."

"I thought maybe a small group of soldiers drugged like him would make an acceptable bodyguard," Lyndon pointed out slowly. "They may have their downside, but they are irretrievably loyal."

"Loyal like a dead duck," Trinity muttered.

Lyndon's eyebrows shot up. "What do you want me to do? Take him off the drug? We don't know what his background was. Get rid of him? Why don't you give orders to the trainers?" he added as an afterthought. "See what you can make of him. See if his type can be useful. He's only had a week of training so far," he reminded her.

Trinity nodded. "Okay. I'll do that." She smiled slowly. "Good, that gives me something to do. I hope it'll be interesting."

* * *

As dusk fell over Annapolis that night, Giulia made her way out of the city, driving her car as fast as was allowed through back roads. She was terrified for her life. If she stayed in Annapolis, she had no doubt but that whoever the plotters were would have no trouble getting her out of the picture. So she was leaving for now.

She had left an anonymous message for the police. She hoped they'd be able to deal with the situation. But she wasn't going to risk her life waiting around to make sure. That was something for the police, not an ordinary civilian like her. And for now she'd probably have to stay on the run. Giulia had no intention of getting murdered.

* * *

It was a few days later, when Nina Marwick was at work, that her team got a call that there'd been an accident a few streets away. They reported to the scene immediately, in their ambulance. Nina and one of her friends rushed over to the cars, where a group of police and firemen already were.

The vehicles had already caught on fire, and the firemen had just managed to retrieve the passengers before the two cars exploded, almost simultaneously.

Nina watched the flames for a moment, as they rocketed sky-high. Then her sense of duty recalled her, and she looked around.

One of the passengers was sitting up, looking dazed; he had a nasty cut on his forehead, but otherwise he looked alright. Nina and her friend ran over to the other passenger, and Nina gasped.

"It's Mrs. Whyte!"

* * *

Moira didn't hear the news till a few hours later, when her dad called her on the phone. The police had called him in Washington, and he'd been told. Now it was his turn to pass the news on to Moira.

"She's at the hospital, in a coma, they said," he'd told her, while Moira listened, dumbstruck. "I'll be in Annapolis tomorrow—but I can only stay one day. I wish it could be longer, but it really can't. The White House is worried about some goings-on, and I need to be here whenever possible. I'm going to see if I can get someone to let you stay with them till Mom's better. Moira, are you there?"

"Yeah," she'd replied softly.

"You're gonna have to be brave. I know you can handle this, Moira. I hate how I'm never home, but you know how things are with my kind of job," he'd reminded her.

"Yeah, I know," Moira had whispered. She hated how her father worked in the government. It was never fair on the rest of them. But Victoria Whyte wouldn't leave Annapolis for anything.

"Sure you can spend the night there on your own?"

Moira had spent that night hacking. Well, most of it; until two in the morning. She'd gotten so far, and now she was being asked for a password to clear the firewall. She had a list of combinations she'd already tried. It had about a thousand entries already. But now Moira was struggling against giving up, not a random collection of coding. The password could be literally anything.

There was one thing that told her she was on the right track. It was asking for a Violet Encephalon Passcode. And that word, Violet, seemed so intrinsically connected with the whole mystery that she clung to it as proof she was working the right way. All she had to do now...was discover the password.

Adrien had arranged it so that she could stay with the Marwicks, since she wanted to stay where she could visit her mother often. Moira packed the computer carefully, and set it up in Cloe's room, which had been evacuated for her use. Every minute of her spare time, she was hacking. And when she wasn't hacking, she was visiting her mother, who was still at the hospital.

Victoria was still in a coma, though the doctors didn't know why. Everything else was healing well and rapidly. Moira sat by her mother's side almost every afternoon after school, wishing, hoping, and praying desperately that she'd get better. But it helped that Victoria wasn't dead. Moira still had a scrap of hope to cling to.

Like she did with her twin.

twenty-two

____2 MONTHS LATER____

"Moira, volleyball?" A tall, blond-haired girl of fifteen, by name of Clotilde Marwick, aka Cloe, popped her head into the room that had formerly been hers—but not for the last two months.

Moira Whyte was hacking away as usual at the desk in the room. "Busy," she replied briefly, without even looking around. Yet as she said it she sighed.

But Cloe wasn't going to give up that easily. "Come on," she persisted, as an impatient tone crept into her voice. "You've been in here every single day of Thanksgiving break. And the weather's perfect for volleyball right now, and the girls all agreed to do it. We've got school tomorrow. If you don't come play today, our team will lose again and it'll be all your fault."

Moira sighed again, louder this time. "This is hopeless," she admitted.

"Then come on and play!" Cloe repeated.

"Wait..." Moira muttered, typing something quickly into the *Type Password Here.* Her screen turned red for what was about the millionth time. *Incorrect.*

Moira nearly screamed in frustration, and pushed her chair back suddenly, standing up. She turned off her monitor and grabbed Conner's—now presumably Moira's—coat from the back of her chair, and followed Cloe out of the room.

"What did you try?" Cloe whispered to her as they went into the hall together.

"'Come on and play,'" Moira whispered back.

"What!" Cloe exclaimed, laughing.

Moira shrugged. "I'm totally out of ideas!"

Nina was by the front door, tossing her car keys from one hand to another. "Ready to go? Good, you got Moira." She nodded approvingly at her younger sister.

"Yeah, but she was a pain," Cloe complained, giggling. Moira glared at her.

Nina shrugged. "Come on, girls; let's go."

* * *

"Did you guys forget how to play?" Nina was lecturing her team about forty-five minutes later. "Come *on*, guys! We can do better than this! Why are you all acting half asleep?"

The other girls on her team just stared without really answering. But one of them mumbled something about the whole thing's being a waste of time. Nina stared. It wasn't like her friends at all.

"Lucinda?" Nina came over to the net. "Is there something wrong with your team, too? Though you've won every one of the three games we've played."

Lucinda shrugged. "I dunno. Hey, girls!" she shouted at her team. "What's up?"

"Victory." Cloe grinned.

"Death from natural causes. I mean, thirst." Moira started running over to the shaded school entrance. "I forgot my waterbottle—I'm going to get a drink!" she yelled back.

Nina, Cloe, and Lucinda sat down under a tree. The other girls eventually crowded over to the other side of the court, where they sat down, generally just sitting silently. The Marwick girls and Lucinda watched them for a few minutes.

"It's so weird," Cloe whispered. "They're acting like zombies. So unresponsive. I'm getting goosebumps."

"I'd think they were sick," Nina commented thoughtfully, "but they aren't really acting like it..."

Lucinda laughed, sounding slightly annoyed. "*I* should be acting like that, if anyone," she admitted. "My allergies have been really bad in the past few days."

Cloe looked at her, intrigued. "What are you allergic to again?"

"Bees and fluoride," Lucinda replied. "And I've been breaking out worse than ever whenever I get a drink of water, so I've been sticking to orange juice instead; that's why I was well enough to play volleyball today." She sneezed. "Maybe they've been putting more fluoride in the city water lately."

Further conversation was cut short by the imminent arrival of Moira, who was running back to join the group. She had an utterly annoyed look on her face as she sat down between Lucinda and Cloe. "The water in there tastes absolutely disgusting," she reported.

Lucinda pulled a face. "Really?"

"Yeah." Moira coughed, as if to rid her mouth of the taste. "Anyway. What's up with them?"

"No idea," Nina told her, shrugging. "It makes no sense to me. I just can't put my finger on it."

"Hey, Moira," Lucinda broke in. "How's the hacking going?"

Moira scowled. "Just as badly as ever. The only hint it's giving me is 'Roses aren't always red.' That's obvious!" she fumed. "I wonder what the person who came up with that was thinking!"

"But rose-colored roses are red," Lucinda pointed out dryly.

"That's irrelevant," Moira retorted, closing her jaw with a snap. Lucinda shrugged.

"Roses are red, Violets are bl—" Cloe began mumbling.

Suddenly a brainwave hit Moira. "Wait! Cloe, say that again," she demanded, standing up.

"Everyone knows that poem." Cloe blinked.

"Yeah. Yeah, you're right." Moira sounded somewhat distracted. "Roses are red, Violets are blue, Sugar is sweet, And so are you. Roses are red, Violets are blue, I've got it!" she yelled exultantly, jumping into the air.

"Got what?" Lucinda asked her, staring.

"See you guys later!" Moira took off at a flying run down the street.

"And this," Lucinda commented as they all stared after her in surprise, "is why you don't spend all day staring at a computer screen." They laughed.

"I wonder what she thinks she has," Cloe murmured.

twenty-three

Later Moira would remember that run as an absolutely crazy dash of three miles, but in her present mood it was nothing. She reached the Marwicks' house at length, and stumbled in through the front door, feeling completely exhausted. But the first thing she did there was rush to her room and turn on her monitor. She shifted balance from her right foot to her left and repeated, waiting for the slow screen to finish turning on. But finally it did, and she was back at the page that asked her for a password.

She already knew what she was going to put. Quickly she typed it in.

Violets_are_purple!

Moira crossed her fingers, holding her breath as the submission processed. It took three times as long to load as it normally did, and intuition told her that she'd been right. Still she held her breath, with the feeling that if this was wrong she'd just give up forever.

But the screen flashed green. She was right!

Moira sank weakly into her chair, exhaling loudly.

"Oh thank heavens," she managed to gasp out.

Passcode correct. Taking you to Encephalon Login...

Then the screen changed again. Moira pushed her exhaustion aside to lean forward and read it. It said *Encephalon Login* and asked her for a username and password.

"Okay, scrap that," Moira muttered, staring. This was hopeless. Totally hopeless.

She tried a few things, then stood up from her desk and went to go get a cup of drinkable water from the filtered faucet in the Marwicks' kitchen.

Maybe she'd figure it out later, but now...

She came back with her cup, and sat down at her desk. But when she looked at her screen, her jaw dropped open.

She'd been signed in.

Welcome, Lyndon Arnnu, it told her. She sat there gawking at the display in surprise.

The website, or whatever it was, was made up of various shades of purple. Not for the first time, Moira reflected that whoever was doing this was obsessed with the color. Leaning forward, she started to read. There was a list of links to other sites, with strange names that definitely caught Moira's attention: *Campaigns, Contacts, Studies, Research, Encephalon Command, Violet, Personal.* Moira scanned over them a few times, and her brow furrowed. Shrugging, she clicked the first link: *Campaigns.* She gasped as it brought her to another list, beginning with *Annapolis Campaign* and continuing with other strategic American cities located all over the country. She clicked *Annapolis Campaign,* and was shocked to see a progress bar at the top of the next page: *Cycle One: 97% Complete.*

The entire page was filled with a complete description of the plan that Encephalon was using to take over control of the formerly American city of Annapolis, capital of Maryland. She read about drugging the city water with some kind of LVED, marching in, shooting civil authorities, and so on.

At the end, she found a list of names.

Annapolis Leader: Violet Arnnu / Trinity Ryder

Bodyguard Officers: Trooper A1, Louis Staunton, Reina Patterson

Click Here to View Garrison

Moira sat back to think the whole thing over. Everything she'd read completely overwhelmed her. The part about drugging the water clicked. That must have been why the water at the school tasted so disgusting! It was from the city water source. And the Marwicks filtered their water, that she knew. That would explain why everyone she knew lately had been looking more and more out of it all.

She realized that if these Encephalon people were starting with Annapolis, then likely the leader here would be in charge of the whole operation. The names for the leader were linked, so she clicked on *Violet Arnnu* first.

She got a much friendlier-looking webpage, headed by a photo of a young girl, perhaps twelve or thirteen, dated 8/3/17. Moira leaned close to study it. The girl had been riding a bicycle, complete with pink and purple streamers on the handles; it was tilted, and one foot was on the ground instead of the pedal. She was wearing bright pink rompers. It was a sunny day in what looked like one of the more westerly states to Moira. She was smiling brightly, exposing two lines of sparkling white teeth, though there was one missing in the front. Her short, curly hair was a lovely, rich tone of dark brown, and her bangs had been braided to hold the rest of her hair out of her face.

But what was most striking was her purple eyes. And the happy gaiety shining in them. Moira had a feeling that she would like to know this girl. But then she noticed the year, and made a quick mental count. This Violet Arnnu person would be about nineteen now: three years older than Moira. Moira shrugged.

Then followed a series of other pictures, each one taken of the same girl and marked *Happy Birthday*, with the links *School* and *Training* following most of them. Using the pictures, Moira could trace her up to when she turned thirteen. Then the page ended abruptly, with only a link leading to *Trinity Ryder*. Moira clicked it.

It was the same girl, but this page was more of a personal website, starting with a picture of Violet as an older teenager, headed *Trinity Ryder*. Moira studied this one carefully as well. It was definitely the same girl as in the previous webpage. But she was probably eighteen in this photo, and the tips of her dark brown hair were dyed a light purple. It was much longer now, and her bangs fell down all the way to her cheeks. Her purple eyes looked even more purple now, and almost dreamy.

Moira went on reading, but this was all obviously stuff Trinity Ryder had organized herself. There was a *Life Story* in the first person, and other things, like a link to Twitter. None of which was what Moira was really looking for—why was this person taking over Annapolis, and the United States?

Confused, Moira went back to the Annapolis Campaign webpage, and hit the next linked name. What she saw there gave her what she'd always consider the closest reaction to a heart attack. She literally stopped breathing.

The two pictures there. Beyond doubt, they were of Conner. The first one made Moira want to cry. He was unconscious, strapped to a chair, with an IV taped onto his wrist. And the second... She didn't know what to think about the second. He was taller. Stronger. In a purple soldier's uniform.

Standing straight and tall. But it was still him, though his dark eyes were hauntingly devoid of expression.

They were labeled, *Trooper A1.*

Moira stared for a long moment, then exhaled in a long, shrill whistle.

So she'd been right. Her twin was alive.

What had happened to him?

She scrutinized the second picture again. He looked so strong and healthy that Moira smiled in spite of herself.

But why on earth was he wearing a soldier's uniform? Why was he working for these people? What had changed him? Nothing made any sense!

Farther down the page, she had her answer.

LVED: Yes

Memory Wiped: 27 August 2024

Moira clenched her fists, breathed out slowly, and bit her lip hard. It looked like these people had erased her brother and replaced him with a robot.

She was going to—

twenty-four

"Moira?" Cloe stuck her head in the doorway of her friend's bedroom, about thirty minutes later. "You okay?"

Moira jumped; she'd forgotten to close her door, she realized now. She spun around to look at Cloe. "Where's Nina? Is she home?"

"Yeah, I'm here," came a voice from down the hall.

"Can you two please come in here and look at this?" Moira demanded urgently, going back to the very top of the first website.

The words came out all in a rush. "I found Conner. And someone is taking over Annapolis and the USA. Nina, who do we tell?"

"Uhh, Moira, you're kidding me, right?" Nina stared. "This is crazy. What's up on your screen?" she added as an afterthought.

Moira pushed her chair back and stood up. "Wanna see? It's all the Encephalon's plans. If you click on 'Campaigns' and 'Annapolis Campaign' you'll see what I mean," she continued as Nina sat down. "And Conner is one of their soldier thingies."

"Conner?" Cloe asked in disbelief. "Conner? A soldier thingy?"

"They wiped his memory and have him on some kind of suppressing drug called LVED," Moira explained. "It's not the Conner we know." She bit her lip again.

"Whoa," Nina exclaimed suddenly from where she was sitting at Moira's computer. "Guys, we gotta tell the police. Anyone got a phone in here?"

"I do," Moira volunteered, grabbing it out of her pocket. "Can I talk to them?"

"Uhh, they might believe us more if an adult talks," Nina pointed out. Moira nodded in recognition, and handed the older girl her phone.

"You aren't an adult," Cloe mumbled to herself as Nina started dialing, but Nina ignored her.

But a few seconds later, she looked up, confused. "It says you need to switch service, or something," she reported to Moira.

"That makes no sense...wait. Oh no." Moira stepped over to her computer and refreshed the webpage. She turned white.

Cycle One: 100% Complete. Initiating Cycle Two...

The time was 4:00 pm December 1, 2024.

"Oh no," Moira repeated. "Oh no. We're too late."

"Too late?" Cloe repeated, staring at her older friend. "What do you mean, too late?"

"I'll tell you," Moira replied absently, turning off her screen and running out of the room. She ran down the hall towards the front door, which she threw open. Cloe and Nina followed. And Jack came out of his room and stood in the doorway behind them.

That was the exact moment when the loudspeakers started blaring. Loudly enough to be heard all throughout their section of the city, inside and outside. Cloe cringed and covered her ears.

"Citizens of Annapolis." The voice was that of a young woman, though it was slightly marred by the speaker quality at full volume—or the lack of said quality. "This day marks the beginning of the Violet Empire. Annapolis is the first to be incorporated into the Empire. Congratulations.

"My name is Trinity Ryder, and I am now your ruler. I want to warn you that any type of resistance will not be tolerated. None of it has a chance, as probably most of you know already." A laugh. "This invasion is not new; it began here a week ago, and now it is finished.

"Your first orders are to turn in your weapons, electronic devices, food, and stored water. You are to bring them to the city square by sunset tonight. There will be rations sent out daily from now on."

Moira saw that literally everyone else on that street who'd come outside now darted back inside to follow the command. The woman wasn't joking. Everything was under control.

"Tonight there will be a search. Anyone who has failed to comply will be shot on the spot.

"The Violet Army is at this very moment exterminating the police and the students and teachers of the naval academy here. Anyone caught harboring them will suffer the same fate.

"I know a few of my audience are extremely confused right now," the voice continued, and Jack jumped. "Why should you listen to these orders? Why is everyone else listening? You'll find out soon. Meanwhile, if you don't listen, you'll be shot as well. I know who you are."

Moira's face paled slightly as she listened.

"I will be watching you. My army is superhuman; you have no chance. I strongly advise you to behave. Or you won't find out how this ends."

Moira was clenching her fists now. But then she heard a droning sound from above, quite faint at first, but growing louder. She looked up.

There was a small black speck coming out of the clouds now, coming straight down, towards the intersection a little ways down the street. As she and her friends kept watching it, they realized it was a drone.

"Everybody inside," Moira hissed to the others. "And make sure the windows and everything are closed."

* * *

"Are you ready, Trin?" Lyndon glanced up as his daughter walked into the room, and he smiled. "Amazing. Nobody can stop you from following your destiny, Vi. Only you can write your future."

Trinity smiled.

She wore a complete and personalized battle suit. Her dark purple jacket, with a high collar, was only partly zipped up, and at her waist was a belt which held a handgun and other combat equipment. Her gloves and tights were of light purple, and her boots were a very dark violet. On her face she wore wraparound goggles complete with microphone and earpiece, tinted purple. Over her shoulders was draped a short cape of the lightest purple imaginable. Her hair was loose and free as usual.

Her smile? It was excited and proud. Behind her were her three personal bodyguards—the best-trained of all the Violet Army: Trooper and two others. They wore soldier outfits that were much like Trinity's, but they wore full helmets and no capes.

"Is it time to pick up the pen?" Trinity asked softly.

Lyndon nodded, his smile growing wider. "Yes. It's time."

twenty-five

Even as Nina, the last to go in, locked the door behind her, the speech was still going on. They could hear it from inside, but now they could semi-ignore it, pushing it back into the subconscious of their minds.

"I now address myself to the world. Be aware that you will also be invaded and that there is no way to stop us. If you want to spare your countries excess bloodshed and suffering, I strongly advise you to surrender to me immediately. Yes, I know the proposal seems ridiculous. I give you until I will have finished my conquest of the United States to decide..."

Moira drew a deep, shuddering breath. "And that," she addressed Nina, Cloe, and Jack, "is what I meant by too late."

"Will someone please explain to me what on earth is going on?" Jack demanded.

"That Trinity Ryder person is trying to take over the world, starting with Annapolis, and they've finished here," Moira told him briefly. She glanced at Nina. "Do we have anywhere we can hide my computer—oh, and my dad's gun he always leaves at home? I'll run and get it if we do. Wait, where are your parents, again?"

"Out of state," Cloe whispered, suddenly realizing that this meant they were all on their own. "They're visiting Grandma."

"Oh, joy," Moira muttered. "Perfect timing. Nina?"

"Why are you trying to hide this stuff?" Nina asked her levelly. "To get us all shot?"

"No!" Moira retorted, taken aback. "I can hide them at my house if you like. But if we don't do something, the entire world is in trouble!"

"What? Why?" Jack asked, looking unnerved. The girls ignored him.

"Moira, we can't possibly do anything," Nina told the younger girl quietly. "We're teenagers. All four of us. Our Mom and Dad aren't home, and neither are yours. This is suicide."

"Do you know what they intend to do with the world?" Moira returned, trying to keep calm although her voice was rising. "Do you? No! But I read more about it than you did. And I know! They're going to wipe out the millions of people who are impaired or defective in any way, and inject the remainder with the same thing they've given their army. They're going to turn the entire world into super strong people! But over the slaughter of millions! Do we want that?"

"No!" Cloe replied energetically.

Nina shook her head. "That doesn't change anything, Moira. Yes, that's a terrible thing to do, but we can't stop it!"

"But we are the only ones who can!" Moira shouted. "No one else knows what they're up against! No one else knows their plans! Nina, we're the *only* ones who can!"

She spoke passionately, her face and dark eyes speaking volumes of emotion. In the face of such determination, Nina began to back down. But she did not reply.

"And," Moira continued, "and they have Conner."

Nina threw her arms in the air. "How does that help us? Moira—you're not doing this for the world, you're doing it for yourself. You want Conner back. A leader can't fight for herself. She has to fight for others!"

"We have to fight for the world. And the world includes Conner. Besides, I'm not the leader," Moira returned swiftly. "You are! You're the only adult here!"

"Me!" Nina exclaimed. "Are you kidding? I have no idea what you even want us to do!"

"Right now, we need to hide my computer and a gun. Or even just the computer. And then we need to get our food, water, other devices, and weapons over to the square," Moira went on, gaining momentum. "We need to make sure they're aware that we aren't under the drug's influence."

"Why on earth—?" Cloe gesticulated helplessly. Jack was just totally lost at this point.

"You'll see," Moira shrugged. "But Nina! Where do we hide my computer? It needs to be somewhere I can work on it."

Nina still had no clue what Moira was trying to do, but she had no choice but to give in. "How about—"

She was interrupted by a deafening roar from outside. "TO STRENGTH!"

All four of the teenagers jumped.

"And that was—?" Jack mumbled.

"The Violet Army," Moira shrugged. "Come on, guys, we're running out of time. Let's get this going!"

* * *

"You're all good. Food goes that way." The Violet Army Inter pointed toward an ever-growing mountain of various containers of food.

"Okay," the person replied, walking off.

The Inter motioned to the next person in line, a tall brunette carrying nothing but obviously just waiting to put her name on the list. "Next!" the Inter shouted.

"Have you got my name yet?" the girl asked, pushing her hair out of her face with one tanned hand.

"No." The Inter could tell right away from looking at her eyes that she wasn't on LVED, and made a note accordingly. "What is it? And I need your age, and DOB, and your parents' names, unless you're eighteen."

"It's Moira Whyte." She hesitated. "Do you need my middle name?"

"Yeah?"

"Moira Bernadette Whyte, then. I'm sixteen," Moira added, watching the Inter's fingers fly across the keyboard. "My birthday is January 3rd. And my parents' names are Adrien Whyte and Victoria Smyth Whyte. I—is that good?"

"Their names aren't on here," the Inter complained.

"Dad works out-of-state, and Mom's in the hospital," Moira explained, watching the Inter's face anxiously for approval.

"Do you have an SS card or a driver's license?" was the next question.

"I've got a learner's," Moira shrugged. "But it's at home."

"Well then. Where do you live? If your parents aren't at home?" He fixed his glare on her.

Moira didn't miss a beat. "With some friends." She gave the address.

"What school do you attend?"

"Annapolis High School," Moira supplied.

"One moment..." The Inter clicked a few things on his laptop, and then the printer next to him started up, spitting out a purple band. The soldier checked the information on it against what he had on the computer, and nodded.

"I need your right wrist," he told Moira, who lifted her right arm, pulling the sleeve of Conner's coat back a bit. The Inter snapped the band around it, tight enough that it wouldn't slip off.

"Don't try to make that come off," he warned her, "because it won't. One more thing. I need you to press your fingerprints down on this." He gestured toward a finger pad, and Moira complied.

"What's the band do?" she asked while her prints processed, though she already knew.

"That's none of your business," the soldier replied shortly, making final adjustments on his computer.

"Is purple special or something?" Moira pressed, inspecting the band. Printed on the outside were her name, DOB, and a number. On the inside, she knew from her research, was a locator, shocker, and pulse detector.

He gave her another queer glance, but ignored her question. "You're good to go," the soldier told her instead of responding.

"Mhmm," Moira nodded, walking off as quickly as she dared. She met up with the Marwicks and Lucinda some distance away on a bench outside the high school building. They'd let Lucinda into the secret. All four of Moira's friends already had their bands, and as Moira approached, Cloe stood up.

"Are you sure these things aren't recording everything we're saying?" she asked Moira anxiously, leaning forward to whisper directly in her friend's ear.

"I'm sure." Moira nodded confidently. "It wasn't listed. There's no way to access any type of recordings from the website except pulse and location, and besides, they wouldn't have enough people to listen in on all these."

Cloe smiled. "Okay, good. Because Jack keeps wanting to take his off."

Moira raised her eyebrows. "Don't do that," she told Jack. "They'll self-destruct. And I know it won't kill you, but believe me, it'd probably take your hand off."

The boy shuddered. "Okay. Okay. I'll forget it."

"Good," Moira grinned.

Nina had had a faraway look in her eyes as the younger teenagers talked, but now she seemed to snap back to attention. "Moira, what happens next? The rations they give us will be drugged."

"I know," Moira nodded, "but only the water will be. It's too expensive to drug the food, and water is more essential anyway. That's why we have a few plastic bottles hidden, remember?"

"Yeah, but what happens when that runs out?" Nina returned, point-blank. "We only have one bottle each for the five of us. It won't last long."

"I know," Moira told her patiently. "It'll start snowing any day now. So we'll be fine."

"Wait, the five of us?" Lucinda spoke up. "What about my family?"

Moira looked at her seriously. "They're already on LVED. It's only you who aren't, because of your allergies... Besides, the responsibility in this is ours, and ours alone."

"What responsibility?" Jack spoke up. "The trouble we'll get into for hiding a computer?"

Moira shook her head energetically. "No. The responsibility for the world's safety!"

twenty-six

Late that night, after the Marwick house had been searched, Moira retrieved her computer from underneath the back porch, using the darkness as a cover. She brought it back inside, safe in its strongbox. She and the Marwicks gathered in the walk-in pantry, the only room downstairs that didn't have any windows. While she plugged the computer into an outlet and started it up, they discussed the next steps.

"We have to get copies of the plans to Washington, and the European Union, and wherever else," Moira enumerated vaguely. "And we don't have a lot of time for that, either. We can't email anything, or anything like that, and this website is the only thing that works on internet now—the only thing that I've tried, at least. We'll have to make copies...by hand, I guess." She sighed.

"What, you mean like write it on paper?" Jack asked. He was still trying to figure out exactly what was going on.

Moira sighed louder. "Yes. You know, what they did in the days before computers. I'm gonna stay up late tonight and type up an outline. We have to go to school tomorrow, but when we have to work on this as soon as we get back. I'll try to make it as short as possible. And I'll see if Lucinda can come over. I bet the new rules won't allow that, but we'll see," she surmised.

"What then?" Cloe wanted to know.

"Then, once we've finished, we have to smuggle the copies out somehow. Preferably without getting ourselves caught." Moira closed her eyes pensively. "I hate to say this, but we might have to wait until the Enci—" her pet word for the Encephalon "—has had some more success. While it's just Annapolis, they can watch the borders pretty well. We'll have to wait until they're more stretched. Oh, yay, it's finally on." The last was a reference to the computer.

Moira went quiet for a few minutes, getting herself back onto the webpage. Before powering it off, she had taken every precaution that she'd be able to log back on. Even so, she was immeasurably relieved when it actually worked.

"How far are they now?" Nina asked quietly.

Moira frowned. "Annapolis is marked as finished. The Capital is next, with a LVED status of 45%. Baltimore and Easton as well."

A stunned silence.

"Does that mean the U.S. is going down?" Cloe whispered finally.

Moira shook her head. "No, of course not. They have yet to deal with the Army!"

* * *

"The President doesn't know what to make of our ultimatum," Hilton was telling Lyndon and Trinity at that very moment. "However, it's obvious he isn't even considering surrendering the entire country, and I can't blame him," he added frankly. "He already tried land forces, and we beat him off easily. Data gathered from our drones implies that he intends to drop paratroopers from aircraft, early tomorrow morning."

Lyndon chuckled, sounding satisfied. "But we're ready for that. Anything else?"

"There are only about a hundred civilians here in Annapolis who weren't under LVED, but they all cooperated," Hilton reported. "In a week or so there won't be even that. But we're assigning a drone to each of them to be sure, until that time is out. That all right?"

"I expect so." Lyndon shrugged easily. "We have a surplus at the moment. Is mass production of LVED working out well?"

Hilton nodded. "Beautifully. We'll have enough to cover the entire U.S. by the end of the week."

"Very good then," Lyndon smiled.

He turned to Trinity. "You should probably go get some rest now. You won't want to be tired tomorrow. It'll be a big day!"

Trinity laughed, but there was a shadow under her eyes that told that she'd been up since five that morning. "That's a good idea. I'll see you in the morning, Dad."

"Goodnight, Empress Trin," Lyndon told her, his voice gentle and quiet.

"Goodnight, Dad," Trinity smiled slightly, and swept gracefully out of the room.

* * *

Moira stayed up later than Trinity. She was up till three, when she finally decided she had a summary complete enough to satisfy anyone, anywhere. Carefully re-concealing her computer, she crept upstairs to bed, tiptoeing so as not to awaken anyone else. She'd never felt so utterly exhausted before, and her fingers ached. But her mind was so crowded with the climactic events of that day that she found it harder to sleep than she'd ever suspected was possible.

Now, as nothing but the pale moonlight shone through the filmy window curtains, her duty toward country fulfilled for the time being, Moira's thoughts turned to her twin.

Where was he now? What was he doing? Enci work, no doubt, but...

Was there any way to get him back? To himself?

She'd seen a formula to undo the effects of the LVED, though she didn't have the means to make it herself. But even if they managed to reverse Conner's LVED, then...

What then? Was there a way to get his memory back, too? But how could they even get to him?

Moira sighed, and rolled over, burying her face in her pillow. She was desperately thirsty. But she and the others had agreed not to open their bottles of water until the next morning, so she'd have to wait...

Some gray storm clouds drifted over the moon, darkening the sky almost imperceptibly. When the moon shone down unhampered once more, Moira was fast asleep.

twenty-seven

As the moon rolled into view over Annapolis, so did three U.S. aircraft, flying high and silent. Top-quality binoculars were trained on the city, presenting the viewers with a picture of perfect peace and serenity. The planes were silhouetted as black shapes blocking out the stars, their reflections glancing ever so slightly off the shimmery, rippling surface of the harbor's water.

Two of them continued after their first, high pass, but the third curved over a couple of miles, cutting their engines upon approaching the city once more to make a low pass. It was a light three-seater; its pilot, a tall blonde, maneuvered it skillfully in a losing-altitude glide over the city, just skimming the treetops of northern Annapolis before bringing the engines back into action.

They kicked in just in time with a muffled roar, and the pilot brought the plane up into a steep curve, turning the small aircraft nearly sideways. She and her two passengers held on gamely until the plane was mostly righted again, tilted to allow another sweeping pass.

"Are you two ready?" she called to her passengers, keeping her eyes glued to the control panel and her hand wrapped around the controls.

"Absolutely," one replied for the both of them, tightening her parachute straps a notch. She was short, with a sharp nose, olive skin, and dark eyes and hair, giving her a rather Middle Eastern look. Now she stepped closer to the as-yet unopened bay doors. Her friend, the other passenger, followed suit.

"Good," was the quick, brief reply. "I'm going to go high. You can drop a bit before opening your parachutes."

"Right," the third woman nodded. This one was a redhead, her pale face covered in freckles. Her hair was tied back neatly in anticipation of the drop.

Now, as they zoomed toward Annapolis a third time, the other two planes came back into view, finishing a longer loop. Passing the smaller plane, the two larger ones cut a straight course over Annapolis while the last made a leisurely curve. But Annapolis was aware of their presence, and suddenly the loud rat-tat noise of heavy antiaircraft fire sounded. But this AA fire was something unprecedented. It lit up the sky like a rocket as it shot straight up, and then leveled out, honing in on the tails of the two planes. Both were hit, and in the instant that followed, they lit up momentarily with dazzling brilliance. Then, electrified and fried from nose to tail, they made sharp dives straight down into the water.

In the last plane were simultaneous gasps of awe and horror, and the pilot veered to the right quickly, to keep out of range. For a moment there was silence. But the plane was speeding away.

"Wait, go around again," the Middle Eastern woman spoke up suddenly, putting her gloved hand on the lever to open the door.

The pilot's voice was shrill with frustration. "Are you insane, Liszt! Didn't you see what happened just now? Their rockets or whatever...followed the planes like torpedoes!"

Joyce Liszt nodded. "Yeah, I know. But French and I have to get down there." The Irish girl, Erin French, nodded in turn. "Take the plane high, above the clouds. They won't shoot if they don't see anything."

"This isn't a kamikaze plane," the pilot muttered, but still she brought the controls around to make a loop.

"Thanks," Joyce grinned by way of return. She glanced at Erin. "You feeling up to this?"

"Is it dark?" the Irish girl returned, laughing recklessly. It was obvious that she lived for this kind of excitement. All the pilot could do was click her tongue, but not derisively. She was also a pro at handling crime, and had chosen it for her lifetime career.

The plane shot up through the clouds, with the pilot straightening it out a few seconds later to make the final pass.

Then they were gliding. They knew they were over Annapolis, though they couldn't see it through the clouds.

"It's time," the pilot announced.

Joyce pulled the lever, and the bay doors opened. "Come on, Erin, let's jump," she told her friend, suiting action to the word and jumping into the soft, cloudy blackness a moment later.

Dropping downward at an ever-increasing rate might have been terrifying for some, especially at two in the morning, but Joyce happened to love it.

She loved the cold, nearly freezing wind of early December, and dropping through thousands of feet of it so fast took her breath away—literally. But it was only a few split seconds she had for analyzing her thoughts. Now it was time to get to work.

Both women were still free-dropping, not having pulled their parachute straps yet. They were coming out of the clouds now; Joyce could tell because the air wasn't so moist anymore. She caught her breath and looked down. These were the decisive seconds. Would they be seen—or detected?

Down below she could see the twinkling city lights. Apparently these Violet people weren't afraid of being bombed. Maybe because they knew that they had the upper hand with their city-full of hostages? Or they knew it would be impossible to avoid. Whatever the reason, the city was shining like an unclouded sky.

Beautiful, she thought.

It looked like she was coming down in someone's backyard, though it was hard to see while she was so high. Joyce would have liked to drop longer, because parachutes made her and Erin doubly vulnerable and a hundred times easier to see, but they were running out of time. So she pulled her cord.

The gray material blossomed out, jerking Joyce to a near stop in midair. A north wind caught her, and she was floating slowly downward. She looked up. Erin had followed her example.

But if they took too long to reach the ground, they'd still be easy targets. And Joyce was impatient. She grabbed one of the parachute straps and pulled, so that some air whooshed out of the parachute, and she was dropping faster.

That was when the sky above them began to fill with planes. The U.S. air force was turning out in full strength. Joyce knew that the army and the navy would be doing the same. Rockets whistled upward from the center of the city, but paratroopers were dropping from the planes like rain.

Joyce was grinning her head off. No doubt the surprise attack would end this tiny invasion. Who were the Violets that they thought they could stand up against the U.S., anyway?

She heard a sharp whistling sound as a light streaked upwards, and then the hollow, piercing scream that followed it. Startled, she looked up, as a dozen more projectiles were fired. The shooters below were aiming for the parachutes. Now larger rockets made their appearance as well, targeting the planes. Suddenly Joyce was having second thoughts. What were these weapons, that the world had never seen the like of before!

Then small black shapes spun up into the sky with a whir. After a moment of watching them, Joyce could tell that they were drones. But these weren't the usual drone you'd sometimes play with in your backyard. They were shooting at the paratroopers, and every shot made them careen wildly. The shooting gave Joyce an idea. She fumbled with her belt, jerking her gun out of its holder.

One of the drones was zoning in on her, now. Joyce took the best aim she could, what with her hands trembling. She was a great markswoman at military school, but wartime was something new for her.

She shot before the drone did, and missed. The bullet went wide, and its "kick" pushed her backward. Biting her lip, she cocked the handgun, and shot again. She got knocked back another few feet, but the drone went haywire, spiraling downward. Joyce laughed wildly, feeling a rush of crazy relief.

"Yah! These things can die! C'mon, guys let's—" The shout ended in a shrill scream as the young paratrooper landed in a tree, crashing through the thin canopy branches at the top before grabbing the trunk. Joyce laughed again, loudly, and felt incredibly silly. She'd made it!

twenty-eight

Joyce's parachute fell limply around her like a deflated balloon. Stuffing her gun back into her holster, Joyce grabbed her knife and cut herself free. Then she climbed down the tree, looking all around her and gathering her surroundings. She was in someone's backyard—a small yard, with just that one tree, and a kiddy-pool that was covered up for the winter. The house lights were off.

Joyce knew her instructions. Any paratroopers who managed to get into the city were to do their best to group together and facilitate the attack from the other military divisions. If the attack was sure to fail, then they'd be radioed a code word which meant they were to try to conceal themselves as Annapolis civilians until further notice. Breathing lightly, Joyce checked that her radio connection was stable, got her gun out again, and ducked out of the backyard onto the street.

Holding her gun at the ready, Joyce jogged down the street, rolling her feet from her heels to her toes in every step so her formfitting boots would make as little noise as possible on the pavement. She was surprised to notice that the streets of Annapolis looked relatively deserted. A curfew, maybe?

Suddenly the feeling that she was all alone was banished as she turned a sharp corner and smashed into a Violet Army soldier who was coming the same way. They were both totally startled, and Joyce had just enough time to see that her opponent was a young woman and couldn't have been over twenty. She wore the typical uniform, purple helmet, purple suit, purple boots.

A momentary thought crossed Joyce's mind: *I'm getting so sick of this purple.*

The black-eyed stranger and Joyce pulled up their weapons at exactly the same instant.

Even as they did so, Joyce saw the girl's lips moving, though she couldn't hear the words they formed. The helmet must have been soundproof. But whatever the Violet Army girl was saying, the brief preoccupation of speaking probably saved Joyce's life.

Acting on impulse, the American soldier fired before her antagonist had a chance to, her military instinct targeting the small patch of collar between the presumably bulletproof jacket and the also presumably bulletproof helmet.

Joyce was in the military, and death was nothing new to her. As much as she hated to do it, she forced herself to remove the girl's jacket and put it on with the helmet. Reinforcements would be arriving, and disguise was her only chance behind enemy lines.

* * *

Trinity was bored, a type of bored that could be understood only by one who has also witnessed a battle being fought for them, but only witnessed it through screens and speakers. The Violet Army was winning, indeed, but Trinity wanted to go out and join in the combat.

She stood by the door, chafing idly, with her bodyguard of three stationed nearby. Her father, on the other hand, was enthusiastically watching the screens and occasionally directing the battle by means of radio connection. But now he turned to look at Trinity briefly.

"We've just lost our first," he announced, sighing slightly.

One of Trinity's eyebrows arched up stiffly. "Oh?"

"Not an Inter, though. Just a plain Sensor. However," Lyndon added wistfully, "I would like to see what would happen if an Inter got hit. Would they heal instantly? Would they heal normally? By any chance would there be a complication?" He stroked his bearded chin thoughtfully.

Trinity could only shrug. "I dunno," she replied, glancing impatiently at the screens. "I can't just keep standing here doing nothing, Dad. Can I go out?" she begged, for what was probably the twentieth time so far.

Lyndon frowned. "I don't want you getting hurt—" he began, but Trinity broke in with: "I'm not *going* to get hurt, Dad. It's just really annoying, staying in here while everything is happening outside. I can take care of myself."

Lyndon's face showed that he was considering yielding. And then it cleared. "Okay, fine. But I want you sticking with Patterson, Staunton, and Trooper. You understand?" Trinity looked like she was about to say something, but Lyndon kept going nevertheless. "I know you can take care of yourself. I have no doubt of that. But I want those three around to protect you, just in case. You got that?"

Trinity grinned, and her purple eyes sparkled. "Yup!"

A faint smile crept over Lyndon's face as he watched Trinity turn and fairly skip out of the room, followed closely by Reina Patterson and Louis Staunton. Trooper's face was blank for a moment; then he turned as well, and trotted after the others.

Trinity's playful laugh drifted down the hall to Lyndon's ears. "Keep up the pace, Trooper! 'Cuz I'm not waiting for anybody!"

A dark expression came over Louis's tan face. He was sick of the kid who got treated like a soldier.

***

And so the American attempt to retake Annapolis failed. Over three hundred Americans were lost, but all of the Violet Army but two Sensors survived the battle. Lyndon and Trinity were elated. But there was still a problem: the Americans had succeeded in dropping at least forty paratroopers, and Lyndon's men weren't sure they'd taken care of them all. Trinity was tirelessly enthusiastic, and chose herself to lead a team through the city to hunt them down.

"Come on, guys," she addressed her army of two hundred in a large underground assembly room. Lyndon had taken the rest of the constantly-increasing Violet Army to deal with Washington, DC, leaving Trinity in charge of Annapolis. She was loving it.

"Sensors," she addressed her forty noninjected soldiers, "go to your dormitories and get some rest. Good work." She never hesitated to give praise, especially to inferiors, and this quality made her well-liked among most.

"Inters! Check your suits for any problems and then line up. Trooper, Patterson, Staunton, get over here. Motors, get your units in order, and take roll call. I want to know that everybody is present and correct. Reflex, patrol the Dendrites throughout the city. Target anyone without an identity band, and get me a report right away. Is that clear?" she finished, breathlessly.

"Yah! Hail Ryder!" came the carefully timed and pitched response.

Trinity grinned. "Cool, then. Hop to it!" Brushing a loose strand of brown-purple hair out of her face, she turned to face Trooper, Patterson, and Staunton, who'd come up at her orders. Patterson and Staunton were grinning behind their helmets. Trooper was just watching Trinity carefully, like he usually did, and there was no sign of the dead look on his face disappearing.

Trinity sighed without really realizing it. She liked to be optimistic and buoyant—but how could she with a blank, clueless soldier hanging around all the time?

But she didn't hesitate a moment in giving her orders, remembering that her father had been completely adamant about Trooper staying near Trinity to protect her. Even if it made Trinity feel like the young soldier was some kind of guard dog.

"Staunton, make sure the roll calls come out to the correct sums. Check everyone's identities just in case. Patterson, Trooper, we're going with your group, Patterson. Are they ready?"

"I think so," Reina Patterson responded carefully. She was a tall blonde with a no-nonsense look, who took her task of looking after "Empress Trin's" safety all the way. "Which way do we go?"

"North," Trinity decided after half a moment of thought. "Staunton, take south. Two of the other Reflex can do east and west." She brushed her long bangs out of her face again, perhaps mentally reminding herself to get a haircut, and turned, marching towards the door. "You all can march out when you're ready—I'm going now. Come on, Trooper, Patterson!"

Reina gestured toward her second-in-command to get the troop going, and hurried after Trooper, who was already obediently following Trinity out. A faint scowl crept over her face. She hated being on the same level of authority as a robot person; it was humiliating.

At least he wasn't a Reflex, only an Inter, the lowest ranking Violet Army soldier with an injection. But that didn't mean much, only that he wasn't in charge of a squad like Reina and Louis were. Reina knew that didn't really matter, especially when the Inter in question had been trained by Trinity herself.

It was rumored throughout the Violet Army that if the mysterious Trooper A1 was in complete control of himself he might be even better in combat than their leader. Which could either be a good thing for the Army—or a bad thing, if he turned out to be some upright kid who hated wrong. That could spell disaster, and Lyndon wasn't willing to take the chance.

Besides being slightly jealous of him, Reina had no other thoughts about the approximately seventeen-year-old. She was a practical woman, and didn't bother to waste any time wondering how her colleague came to be there.

Unlike Trinity, who'd skillfully transformed the awkward, useless teenager into a master of martial arts, in hand-to-hand fighting as well as in the expert use of various weapons. She knew the story of how the puny kid had been found downstairs, alone and texting for help. The mystery was: How had he come there, without setting off the security system? *Why* had he come? What had he known about Encephalon?

But, Trinity reflected glumly, there was probably no way to find that out now. Still, she wondered. Who had he been? What was his name? Someday, she told herself, she would have him taken off the LVED. Besides, the teenager was already a killer. He was stuck with them, and when the Violet Empire was established, he would have nowhere to run even if he could do what he wanted. And maybe, Trinity pondered, maybe there was a way to get his memory back as well.

twenty-nine

"Now, Trooper!" Trinity tilted her head to the side, watching Trooper more than the running American soldier he was targeting. Trooper fired, his strong shoulder completely absorbing the gun's kick. It was a perfect hit, and Trinity clapped. "Perfect! This makes five. Let's keep looking!"

She ran down the street carelessly, knowing that Trooper would follow to back her up if necessary.

Running.... With the crisp, chilly wind in her face. This was her personally favorite thing about the whole business.

Trinity had always been a great athlete. She could run mile after mile at a time. But with the injection, all that was fantastically amplified. She could run and run literally forever. It was an amazing feeling, and she completely loved it.

When she and her father had finished the taking-over-the-world project, Trinity decided that keeping in shape would be made mandatory. Daily exercise would be an important part of everyone's life. But that, she realized, already fit in with Lyndon's plan of improving the human race—

Thinking about plans while running wasn't such a good idea for anyone, not even a superhuman. Trinity realized that the next moment when she turned a corner and slammed into a girl a few years younger than she was. The speed she'd been at sent the girl flying, while Trinity barely managed to keep her own balance.

The teenager gave a short yelp of surprise, which died away as she scrambled to her feet, turning around to look at Trinity. Her face paled, and she backed away, staring hard.

Trinity stared back. The girl was most likely sixteen, tall, with light brown hair. She wore a patterned skirt and blouse, as well as a thick blue coat with a hood that looked just a touch too small on her. But what really caught Trinity's attention were her eyes.

They were a lovely, deep dark blue, and Trinity knew right away what they reminded her of. They were Trooper's eyes. But these were much clearer, a detail which told Trinity this girl wasn't on LVED, whoever she was.

But that was no cause for alarm. It would be a full week before everyone in Annapolis was on the sedative.

"I—I'm sorry," the girl stammered, continuing to retreat cautiously.

"It's fine," Trinity told her distractedly, hitting a button on her belt that brought up a report on her armband display.

The girl froze.

Moira Whyte, Trinity read quickly. *1-3-9. #A1374V25.*

"Why are you outside?" Trinity asked, glancing back at Moira.

Moira shrugged. "Am...am I not supposed to be?"

Trinity frowned, making the corners of her eye mask go up ever so slightly. "Haven't you realized there's fighting going on? Get going."

"I—okay," Moira stammered, jumping like she'd been stung. And with that she turned around and shot off. Just as Trooper came around the corner.

Trinity glanced at him, momentarily taken aback by the look in his eyes. It was startling, after having seen the Whyte girl's bright and clear ones.

"Where've you been?" she demanded, looking around.

Trooper shrugged. "I thought I had found something," he explained briefly.

"...Well?" Trinity demanded, as the soldier didn't make to continue.

Another slight shrug. "It was nothing."

"Oh?" Trinity knew that Trooper wasn't one to be curious. So "nothing" was most likely something.

"Someone's back porch got blown up," the soldier replied by way of deeper explanation. "Probably one of our missiles misfired."

"Okay." It was Trinity's turn to shrug now. She looked behind her to see Reina running up. "Well, let's get going!"

* * *

Nina, Cloe, and Jack sighed as they stood in the gaping hole in their parents' bedroom wall and stared out at their backyard. It couldn't have been much worse if the Violet Army had actually been targeting their back porch. At least it hadn't caused a fire. Jack wondered what kind of weapon it was that just blew and did nothing else.

They hadn't realized that the loud noise and shaking of the house at four in the morning meant that they'd been hit. But Moira had already been up, it seemed, and around five, just now, she'd run to wake up Nina and tell her there was a huge hole in the wall. And now she'd disappeared. Nina sighed again, knowing the younger girl would probably be discouraged about losing their computer, to say the least. Nina wondered if she'd finished her summary the night before. And had it been on the computer or on paper?

But secretly Nina was relieved. Now that the computer was gone, she wouldn't be worrying every minute of the day that the Violet Army would find it. That would have been the end of everything for them. Now they had a real chance.

She waved, and managed a half-hearted smile as Moira came running up, puffing for breath. Nina and her siblings stepped back as the Whyte girl firmly planted her hands on the jagged gap and sprung up into the room.

"Hey, Moira," Cloe greeted her. Moira only smiled weakly as she caught her breath.

"Where've you been?" Jack interjected curiously.

Moira shrugged, leading the way out of Mr. and Mrs. Marwick's room via the ordinary door into the hallway. "Places. Nowhere really. But I ran into the big boss herself," she added, dropping her voice level down to a whisper, "unless there's someone that looks just like her." She closed the bedroom door behind Cloe, Jack, and Nina, and looked it over, frowning. "Can we block the draft?" she wondered aloud, pointing down at the space between the door and the floor. "Snow is due for tomorrow, right?"

"I think so. Jack, go find something for the door," Nina commanded. "Cloe, see if we're getting rations today, will you?"

"Sure," Cloe nodded, skipping off, not without casting a curious glance at Moira first. Jack walked off without replying. Nina watched them leave, surprise tinging her face. They never listened to her that quickly.

"Nina," Moira spoke up a few seconds later, catching Nina's attention. "The computer's gone. We have no details now, except what I can remember. What do we do now?"

"What do we do now?" Nina repeated, staring at her. "That's for you to answer, not me. Like I would know?" she added sarcastically.

"You're the adult." Moira shrugged, dropping her gaze to the floor. "Fine, then. I think I remember most of what we were going to write. But on second thought, I think it'd be better if we all memorized it instead of writing it—you, Cloe, Jack, Lucinda, and I. Unless you have another idea?" She met Nina's eyes again.

Nina had known she was determined, but still the fiery look in Moira's eyes startled her somewhat. "Okay, but why would we memorize it?" she had to ask.

"So that when we are out we can email it anywhere," Moira explained. "And in the meantime we can make copies to go in bottles that we can get into the harbor to be washed out to sea, just in case. We should have done that befo—"

She never finished the sentence. Not many things could cut Moira short like that when she was enumerating a plan, but one of those few things was a loud pounding on the front door around sunrise.

"Open the door!"

thirty

Moira would never forget the pang that shot through her as she stood rigid in shock. It was her twin's voice!

She didn't have a long time to be immovable, however. Nina gave a low shout of surprise as someone charged into the door they'd just closed, the door to the Marwicks' parents' room, throwing it open and running straight into them, gun drawn and at the ready.

The attacker was a tall blonde, dressed in full Violet Army uniform, complete with a Reflex badge on the front—a glimmering, sharp-edged knife. Her jaw was hard set, her eyes glittering coldly.

Her gun went off, and Nina fell on top of Moira, screaming. Moira didn't think twice, but stuck her foot out as she fell backwards with Nina on top of her and tripped the Reflex officer, who then fell on top of them both.

Moira was the youngest, shortest, and most agile, and somehow she wriggled out from underneath the two heavier people before either of them could get up; she pounced on the Reflex officer, trying to get her off Nina.

Meanwhile, she could hear Jack and Cloe shouting urgently for help.

"Nina! Moira! Do we open the door?"

Moira couldn't answer; Reina Patterson was much stronger than her, and it was all Moira could do to roll her off Nina and try to keep her on the hallway floor.

"Nina? I need help!" she shrieked as Reina brought her knee up and used it to throw the younger girl off.

Moira grabbed Reina's arm as she fell. Reina stood up, pulling Moira up with her. The Reflex officer twisted her arm neatly and suddenly, making

Moira lose her grip; then Reina caught the girl's arm in turn, holding her in an iron grasp. Moira screamed.

"I'm hit, Moira," Nina panted from the floor; Moira looked at her finally and realized with a burst of shock that her friend was hit in the shoulder. "Get Cloe and Jack out of here!" the young paramedic added, pulling herself to her feet and joining the battle straightaway by stepping on the toes of Reina's boots and smashing the fist of her good arm into the visor of the Reflex's helmet.

Reina let go of Moira to deal with Nina, once she recovered somewhat from the whiplash of having her head slammed back like that. Moira ducked between the two, taking Nina's command seriously and devoting her attentions to escaping. The Enci knew about them, and they were closing in, it seemed. They had to get out!

She hesitated, looking back at Nina locked in a fight with Reina. The paramedic was watching her.

"I'll hold her off, Moira! Just go! Survive!"

Moira bit her lip. And then she saw the chance.

Jumping forward a pace or two, she lunged forward, her nimble fingers closing around the Reflex's second gun, stuck securely in her belt. Moira jerked it free, fitting her hand easily around the handle and trigger as she leapt back, out of Reina's reach.

Reina saw—or felt—the move, and spun around so that Nina was blocking Moira's line of fire. Holding the gun in front of her as her father had shown her at a family shooting barbecue, Moira drew breath in sharply, and lowered her arm tentatively.

"Just run!" Nina's voice cut in, a desperate edge to it. That, as well as a sudden thumping at the front door a few rooms away, and Cloe's scream, decided Moira's next move.

She turned, and tore down the hall for the kitchen. "I'm coming!" she shouted to the younger Marwicks, grabbing the corner of the door-less kitchen doorway and swinging herself around it efficiently.

The Whyte girl found Jack and Cloe together, both leaning against the front door to try and prevent whoever was on the other side from getting through.

Even as she approached, the door was kicked, or worse—it shuddered, nearly popping off the hinges. Cloe stumbled forward, and Jack grunted, struggling to retain balance.

"Where'd you get that?" the boy asked Moira quickly, eyeing the purple weapon in her right hand. To him, it looked more like an air-soft gun than anything else, but this was obviously not an air-soft match. This was chaos, and this was real.

She shook her head, motioning for Jack to get away from the door as she held the Violet Army gun straight in front of her, aiming at the door, ready for whoever would come through it first. Cloe and Jack glanced at each other, then backed her up—literally, by standing behind her. Moira mentally calculated the distance between them and the door and made sure that if the door fell in they wouldn't be under it.

"Where's Nina?" Cloe whispered to Moira. Moira only bit her lip harder.

Another bang, and, without Cloe's and Jack's weight to counter act the impact, the door fell inward. Outside it stood Trooper and Trinity, Trooper on the top step, and Trinity a few feet behind him.

Moira recognized Trooper right away, though his helmet's visor was all clouded up, probably frosted up in the frosty winter morning air. And in that moment she knew she couldn't shoot as she'd planned.

"Charge!" she yelled, running forward into her twin and shoving him aside, and leaping down the steps straight into Trinity.

Trinity wasn't prepared for anything like that, and she stumbled back a pace or two before recovering her balance. Trooper spun around before Moira broke free, and grabbed the girl's shoulder, but quick as lightning Moira jerked herself free.

There was a moment of déjà-vu as her instinct subconsciously took her through the exact same movements she'd used so often before, trying to teach her weaker, shorter brother some defensive moves.

Unfortunately, she had taught him too well, it seemed, and Trooper's reflexes remembered the retaliation pattern. He put his foot out, tripping Moira at the precise second when her jerk threw her off balance. Moira slammed face-down onto the pavement, and her gun flew out of her hand, clattering away.

Trooper grabbed one of his own guns off his belt, and lifted his other hand to push up his fogged visor so he could get a clear shot, but before he could do so, he had to deal with Jack, who'd jumped on him when his back was turned.

"You blind idiot!" the older boy shouted, knocking Trooper off the step and down to the ground, landing heavily on top of him. He pounded away at the soldier, yelling in frenzy: "Can't you see—"

Whatever words may have followed were drowned out by Cloe's healthy scream as she tangled with the athletic Trinity. She had never been so petrified in her life; nor had she ever shrieked so loud. But as it happened, it was probably her terror that saved her, because Trinity contented herself with merely pushing the young girl out of her way. Trooper seemed to be having trouble with Jack Marwick, and Trinity went to help him deal with the boy, not realizing that, a few feet away, Moira was reaching for the gun.

Cloe bounced away quickly from where Trinity had thrown her. Part of her wanted to stay and try and help Jack out, but she was just way too scared right now. And when she saw Moira gesturing to her to run, that's exactly what she did. She took off like a timid rabbit, down the street and away from the chaotic scene at which not a few people were staring. Doubtless some of them could point the way for Trinity later, but right now Cloe couldn't care less about that. She just wanted to get as much distance as possible between her and the abnormally tall Violet Army officers.

The adrenaline was surging through Moira's veins as she seized the Violet Army weapon for the second time in five minutes, grabbing it, yanking it off the ground, and scrambling off the pavement at the same moment.

She was able to take aim again, but her strength failed her again when she saw her twin, so long missing, so tragically refound.

"Conner," she whispered, a lump in her throat, a tear springing to her eye. Her throat was so tight she could hardly breathe. She ran a distance down the street over the space of a minute or so, then paused and looked back again.

She could dimly hear Trinity yelling at Trooper not to shoot as he pinned Jack against the wall of the Marwicks' home. Trooper... She couldn't see his face. His visor was clouded.

She forced herself to stop thinking about her twin. How could she rescue her classmate? Maybe she could take out Trinity—yes, and once she took out the Violet Army leader, she could figure out how to save Trooper as well. Moira seized on the idea like lightning, and started looking for a place she could get a good aim from. The only vantage point near enough to be of any use was the roof of the small, one-story kindergarten she was standing next to. And luckily, there was a ladder right there.

Moira was good on ladders, having been the one to help her mom or uncle with roof repairs for the last three years. And now those climbing skills stood her in good stead. She got up the ladder in no time at all, and somehow got roughly to the center of the flat roof, wet with dew from the previous night that hadn't evaporated yet in the rays of the morning sun. The morning sun that was now bathing the entire city of Annapolis in a bath of golden light.

Planting her feet firmly, at an angle to each other and two feet apart for maximum balance and security, Moira lifted her right hand once again that morning, glad that the sun wasn't in her eyes and she could get a perfect view of the tall, brown-violet-haired leader. Moira held her arm out as straight as she could, telling her pent-up nerves to steady her hand. Slowly her hand stopped shaking, and she took a deep breath, aiming carefully.

Trinity's personalized battle suit had one obvious disadvantage: she wasn't wearing a helmet. And Moira wasn't too stupid to realize that that detail was in her favor.

She leveled her gun, right on target, and moved her index finger from the trigger guard to the trigger itself.

Yes. Yes. She could do this, she told herself, focusing on Trinity with every ounce of her being. If she had to shoot and kill someone to rescue her brother and his friend, then she would.

Now.

Her finger started to curl up, and she held her breath, praying desperately. This was it—

Moira Whyte was in no way prepared for the bullet that seemingly came out of nowhere, tearing its way through her blue coat with ease and thudding right into her chest.

The force of it knocked her back to the very edge of the roof, and she struggled for balance for a couple of seconds, unable to comprehend what had happened. She looked down to see the blue coat staining red, and dropped the purple gun.

She grabbed at her chest and looked up, dimly shocked to be staring directly into her twin's eyes. Trooper was holding a gun, the one that he had shot. His visor was down, and she could see his face, his eyes, clearly.

There was a horrible anguish there. And complete recognition.

That was all she remembered, before falling backward off the roof as everything went black.

thirty-one

Swinging his foot high in what Trinity had called a football kick, Trooper kicked the door with all his might, tearing the strong wooden plank off its hinges and sending it heavily to the floor on the other side. Trooper stared into the hallway, blinking. It was much darker than outside, with the lights off, and it didn't help that his visor was all fogged up, but he could still distinguish the three forms that stood just beyond the door. And one of them had a gun. Aimed directly at him.

Trooper had a moment of the nearest thing to panic a Violet Army Inter could get while on LVED, and stood there frozen.

"Charge!" the leader shouted.

Trooper was shocked the next instant when the figure in the lead—he believed it was a girl—lowered her gun and ran past him, into Trinity. His bodyguard instinct kicked in immediately, and he grabbed the girl by the shoulder, pulling her away from Trinity. The girl retaliated by using a sort of twist to free herself. Trinity had never gone over this exact move with Trooper, but somehow he knew what to do next, and he tripped the girl easily.

Someone jumped on Trooper's back, bringing him down to the ground as he yelled. "You blind idiot! Can't you see—"

The third and last person screamed, drowning out Trooper's attacker's next words. Trooper could assume Trinity was dealing with her—the scream bespoke her to be a young girl. He was busy at the moment, what with the tall, heavy, and muscular teenage boy who'd jumped on him.

"Don't shoot him," Trinity warned him a minute later, as he finally managed to knock the young man off him and get back up to his feet.

"Obviously these kids know something," the Violet Army leader added, more to herself than to Trooper.

The soldier shoved Jack roughly against the wall of the building, holding him at gunpoint. Jack was definitely smart enough not to try anything, now that Trooper had the upper hand. But Trinity motioned for Trooper to stand aside, and she faced Jack, identifying him using her and his wristbands.

"Don't move, John Marwick," she warned, "or you won't have a chance to do anything of the sort, ever again. Trooper, go see what's keeping Patterson, will you? We need to catch the two that got away. And tell Patterson that we aren't shooting them—yet!"

Trooper nodded, lowering his gun and stepping back. He turned around to enter the house, but his eyes just caught the projection above a roof some distance away. Someone was on that roof.

The Violet Army soldier pushed his foggy visor down so he could see clearly. He squinted at the figure on the roof, and though the person was so far away it was quite blurry, he could tell immediately that they were aiming a gun. And he suddenly realized they were aiming at Trinity.

He ignored Trinity's command to go help Reina, and instead he lifted his gun, taking careful aim. But the target was too far away, so, to be sure, he mechanically unfolded his sights from the side of his helmet. Then he used Trinity's favorite shooting technique to finish the roof sniper—he followed his line of fire with his eyes, from the end of his gun to the target itself—himself—*herself*—

He knew her.

He knew that face, that sharp, firm chin. The long, light brown hair that blew around her face, shining a fiery golden in the morning sunrise. Those deep, dark eyes, just like his own.

He knew her.

Everything came flooding back to him in a flash. He stood frozen. Everything. He knew his name. His age. His twin sister's name. The years, months, days leading up to his being... Was kidnapped a good word for it? He remembered. He couldn't move. It was all too shocking.

But he had already pulled the trigger.

His head hurt. Everything hurt. He couldn't take the memories, not this fast. And on top of it all, he had shot his sister.

No. This couldn't be happening. But he could see her, see her falling.

Falling. Like she had been in his dream. No. He could see her. But now he couldn't. She had fallen, down from the roof. Or maybe it was his eyes.

Something was wrong with them; he was seeing flashes of bright, spasmodic light. Surely this wasn't real. But he could hear Moira's scream, faint and agonized. Or was it the high-pitched buzzing in his ears? He was only dimly conscious of his surroundings as his senses left him.

The Violet Army had captured him. They'd made him into one of them. And that was what he was now, part of the group that had killed his older brother right in front of him. He was one of them now. He'd killed people. He was a soldier. And he'd just shot his sister.

Conner felt sick. The headache accelerated. *No. No.*

Moira.

He couldn't breathe. He couldn't think. He could only know. Conner dropped to his knees, the gun slipping through his loose, nerveless fingers and clattering away with a sound that echoed and re-echoed in his ears. He could dimly hear Trinity shouting something to him. He couldn't see. But an image of his twin was fixed in his mind: His twin sister only a few minutes before. The look of shock on her face. The stare.

Moira!

He was screaming something. What it was, he didn't know. Pain flashed through his head. The image flickered, and then evaporated into flashes of a blinding whiteness. He screamed louder and louder as the pain, the shock, the horror, the terror intensified. And then, as he passed out completely, only one thought remained.

This was death.

No. This was worse than death.

thirty-two

Trinity didn't even notice that Jack was seizing the opportunity to bolt after Cloe. The sudden report of Trooper's gun had made her whirl around, and now she stared at the Whyte girl on the rooftop some distance away as she fell off.

Following the line of fire back to Trooper, who was only a few feet away from her, Trinity realized what had happened. Moira had been targeting her.

And Trooper had saved Trinity's life—by ignoring orders.

She stared at Trooper with mixed feelings of shock, surprise, and intense relief. "Trooper!" she shouted. "You saved my life!"

She still couldn't quite comprehend it. The young soldier was trained and drugged to obey her and to obey her immediately and without asking questions. According to that training, Trooper should have gone straight into the house, whether or not he'd seen the sniper, and helped Reina deal with whoever else was in the house—and Trinity would most likely be dead or dying a few seconds later.

But instead, the teenager had actually disobeyed her, which meant he had recovered somewhat from that morning's dosage of LVED. And, upon recovering, he had not done as predicted, and attacked the Violet Army leader, but instead he had done exactly the opposite! Could this mean that he was actually sympathetic to their cause? That if they took him off the LVED he could be like any normal Inter?

But as she watched his face freeze, and him fall forward, she knew the truth instinctively. His function as bodyguard had made him fire the shot.

And he'd seen his sister—but too late—and now his memories were coming back.

She stood still, and watched him, slightly fearful, as he closed his eyes and began to scream. The sound was nerve-wracking—a pure, unrestrained, cry of harrowing pain and torture that came directly from his agonized mind and soul. It cut into Trinity like a knife, and she could actually feel what he was thinking. She shuddered. And then blocked her ears.

She realized dimly that somehow she wasn't even angry, or frustrated, or anything she would've expected to be if Trooper got his memory back like this. Maybe later she would be. But right now there was just pity.

The scream stopped, and Trinity uncovered her ears, still watching Trooper as he fell over completely, unconscious. Finally she managed to collect her thoughts, and she dashed up the steps into the house, nearly running slap bang into Nina, whom Reina had captured and was directing out in front of her at gunpoint. Nina jumped back instinctively upon running into another Violet Army officer, and Reina muttered something under her breath. But Trinity was preoccupied.

"Patterson," she ordered, "get your Reflex bunch out here. John Marwick, Moira Whyte, and some girl got away—the Whyte girl is finished, though. We need to get Trooper A1 to sickbay—he's—" Trinity paused. "He's out at the moment. Was this the only one left in the house?" she asked, glancing at the paramedic. Nina was flushed, and looked exhausted, with a bleeding shoulder and a bruised face.

Reina nodded wearily. "Yes: Nina Marwick. I'll tell my team to get out here ASAP. Anything else?"

Trinity shook her head. Reina noticed that the young leader was looking dazed, and she wondered why.

"Stick around with Marwick and Trooper till your guys get here. I'm gonna head back to Encephalon," she explained. "See ya later," she waved, turning and leaping down the house's front steps, then jogging easily and swiftly down the street.

"No, Trinity, wait! Your dad wants—" Reina started to call after her, then stopped, and sighed in disgust. Trinity was ignoring her. How on earth was Reina supposed to protect Trinity if the teenager kept disappearing!

She looked at Nina, noticing that her prisoner seemed about her own age. There was a flame in Nina's eyes as she stared back, that seemed to say *Go chase her, will you?* Reina shook her head quickly, and pulled her radio into place on the side of her helmet, making sure to keep holding the paramedic at gunpoint. Apparently she was the only one they'd managed to capture.

"You there?" Reina asked her second-in-command. "Yes? Well, good. I need ten Inters out here immediately, and a First Aid crew. And get a few Inters to find Trinity and escort her home, will you?...Yes. I lost her. Quickly, now!"

The Reflex shoved the microphone back, and glanced at Nina. "Let's get going. And if you try anything funny," she warned, "you'll end up not going anywhere, see?"

* * *

"Dad? Dad?" Trinity was speaking into her own microphone, a few blocks away from the Marwicks' home. Her voice was wavery. She was feeling slightly dizzy. It was probably just because she'd been out and about all morning, she reasoned to herself. And she hadn't gotten much sleep in the last forty-eight hours, either.

Finally she could hear Lyndon's voice. There was a lot of static, and the background noise sounded like a literal war, but at least he was answering.

"Vi? Do you need something? We're at the White House right now..."

"There's been trouble here," Trinity began, ignoring the fact that he had called her Vi instead of her preferred Trin or Trinity. "Patterson found a bunch of kids that weren't on LVED and were apparently up to something. And Trooper A1...he passed out suddenly." She was watching her words carefully, knowing that if she didn't, Lyndon would invariably give a certain order—an order she wasn't too keen to hear, not yet. "We're gonna take him and the one prisoner back to Encephalon, get A1 into the med bay, and... I dunno what to do with the prisoner?"

Lyndon's voice, even over the crackly radio, was anxious. "Trin! You don't sound like your normal self. Is everything alright there?"

"Ye—" Trinity started.

"Good! And also, my Inters don't just 'pass out.' What happened there?"

Trinity shrugged, though he couldn't see her. "I think...I think something might've happened with the LVED."

"And he passed out?"

"Yeah. He was screaming." Trinity bit her lip. Would he say it or not? He would.

"If he's got his memory back, you should eliminate him. Immediately."

"Dad, he just saved my life."

"He did what?"

"Saved my life. If he's having problems, I'll keep him contained. Hilton Maughan can fix him, right?" Trinity asked.

"I guess. But look, you have to be careful. I don't want him breaking out, do you understand?" Lyndon's voice was decisive.

"Alright." Trinity hesitated, then finished: "I'll keep him contained."

thirty-three

Moira.

That was the first word that came into his head.

Everything was still.

He was sitting, he realized as he gradually came awake. He was sitting in a chair, his arms and legs strapped so tightly to it that he couldn't move them. He felt a needle in his left hand. He could hear voices in the background, but he didn't open his eyes, just tested the bonds lightly.

He knew where he was.

Where was Moira?

"He's awake now," someone said. "At least, consciously. I don't know if..." Hilton's voice trailed off into silence.

"Trooper? Trooper A1?" This time it was Trinity speaking. Her tone was soft and cautious. "Are you feeling better now?"

He had to open his eyes, and he did. He blinked. There was a bright light shining directly into them, and it hurt. But now someone pushed the light away, and he could see again, though everything was foggy for a few seconds.

Trinity, Hilton, and Trinity's other bodyguard Louis Staunton were there, standing a few feet in front of the chair. Trinity had pushed the light away.

She and Louis were still in their battlesuits—Trinity's with a crimson smear on her right sleeve—and Hilton was decked out in his ordinary scientist laboratory clothes. Conner stared at them.

"Where's Moira?" he demanded, his teenage-boy voice quiet yet strong. His eyes were the clear dark blue they had once been. The clouds were gone. For the first time in weeks, he looked actually alive.

Trinity openly hesitated. "Moira?" she asked doubtfully.

"You don't know a Moira," Hilton broke in sharply, his tone hard and flat. "What are you talking about, A1?"

"Moira," Conner repeated. "My sister. Where is she?"

Nobody answered him.

"If she's dead, I will kill you all," Conner warned, his voice somehow remaining level, calm, and quiet. "Where is she?"

Trinity had to hide a smile. A seventeen-year-old—or maybe sixteen-year-old—strapped to a chair and completely at their mercy—"killing them all"?

But Hilton had seen and heard enough to have his suspicions confirmed, and now he turned, bringing his right index finger to hover over a button on the IV machine close to the chair. But Trinity's voice stopped him.

"No, Hilton. I want to talk to him," she ordered, gesturing gracefully for the scientist to stand aside.

Hilton hesitated. "But your father said—"

"Dad doesn't know everything that happened," Trinity broke in, "and I'm in charge of Annapolis, anyway. So get your hand away from that button, or I'll chop it off," she added vehemently, noticing that Hilton didn't look too keen to obey. "And get away from it," she finished imperiously.

Hilton stepped away, facing the wall so that the bossy eighteen-year-old Violet Army leader wouldn't see the angry red flush that spread over his face. But it was unnecessary; Trinity wasn't even paying attention to Hilton. She was looking carefully at Conner.

"Do you know me?" she demanded.

Conner nodded as far as his bonds would let him. "Yes. I do."

"You know where you are?" Trinity continued.

"Yes."

Trinity's lips curved into a smile. "Good. And you remember everything?"

Conner merely nodded this time.

"Excellent," Trinity approved. "Well then. Some of us want to get rid of you—we think you're too dangerous to keep around. But you saved my life, so I'm giving you a chance, see? Look, you're completely one of us now. You, sir, are a killer. You have killed..." Trinity tried to remember.

"Thirty-two people, including your sister," Louis Staunton finished for her, glowering at the boy.

Trinity was visibly relieved. "Yes. Exactly."

"So she really is dead?" Conner asked, and something in his eyes died.

Trinity nodded as a matter of course. "Well, naturally. Your aim is pretty good," she added. "So. You have no choice but to finish this with us. And if you prove yourself to be trustworthy, we'll set you free, and you'll be just like any other Inter. What do you think?"

"I think not," Conner replied firmly. He shut his mouth tightly.

"Well, I would say you have all the time in the world to start thinking," Trinity told him, "but my Dad will be back here within a couple of weeks. So you have until then to make your choice."

"I've already made it—" Conner began, but Trinity interrupted with: "You can only make one choice, really, if you want to live, and it's the choice that we want. Join us—or die. I'll give you time to think on it," she assured him, marching out of the room, followed closely by Louis and Hilton.

"Never," the teenager in the chair muttered.

***

The days passed slowly for Conner, as they would for anybody who had to spend them bound arms and legs to a chair. He told himself he would stick it out. He wasn't killing any more innocent people; he'd die first. The Violet Army could kill him if they wanted to. If he'd killed Moira, he didn't care anymore.

But still the strain told on him, and he grew increasingly impatient and frustrated. Every waking moment was spent in trying to break free; every moment asleep, dreaming of his past life. Memories of him and his twin together would haunt him; he relived his expedition into the gun shop multiple times; he saw his Trooper self shooting the people he'd murdered, over and over. He would wake up screaming and fighting the bonds; he knew only too well that it was useless, but he fought and fought till he fell asleep of sheer exhaustion...and dreamed again.

It was enough to drive anyone mad, let alone a weak and despairing sixteen-year-old. By the third day he was yelling, screaming alternately threats and challenges to whoever might be listening in, though he was left alone 99 percent of the time.

He hated being alone. The room bare of anything and everything but him, the torturous chair, the IV machine—he hated it with a fury nothing could match. He hated the purple—just looking down at his clothes would turn him absolutely livid. This would end with his going insane, he knew. He wouldn't have cared, if he hadn't realized that if he went insane the Violet Army could twist him to their own evil purposes.

There was nothing to hope for in life, for anyone who had shot their own sibling. There was no one to rescue him, no one to save him. But still he clung to the last remaining shreds of his sanity. He would not let the Violet Army have him, not ever again. He would win. Even if it meant death.

For being a machine was worse than death.

"Encephalon!" he screamed one day. He pulled and pushed at the straps that held him there. "Trinity! Lyndon! You'll never win, I'm telling you! Never!" His voice was cracking, but he screamed the word again anyway. "Never!"

thirty-four

Some distance away, in a small, dark room that looked suspiciously like someone's basement, Conner was being watched. The video display of the safe-room was up on a computer monitor, and there were four people in the room.

One was sitting at the desk, looking carefully at the display; another was delicately fusing a strip of some unidentifiable material to the collar of a damaged Violet Army uniform. The other two were dissecting one of the Dendrite drones, which presumably they had shot down, because the computer insides were a mess of what they were calling shrapnel, for lack of a better word. It was mostly bits of wires, wire protectors, battery, and motherboard, all mushed together, and they weren't able to make much sense from it.

"This is hopeless," one of them declared, shoving a pile of junk away from him on the table with his right hand.

His left hung limply at his side, and a dog—a German shepherd—stood next to him. He was Darek Lasek, the former Annapolis policeman who'd been honorably dismissed from the force after crippling his left hand while chasing after the suspect for the murder of Conner Whyte. Rocky was still with him.

His companion, a young woman whose red hair and freckled face revealed her to be one of the paratroopers, Erin French, nodded dismally. "It's a mess."

"At least this is going better," Joyce Liszt, the other lady in paratrooper uniform, spoke up from her chair where she sat fixing and improving the Violet Army getup she'd captured a few days before.

The fourth and final person, who was actually Erin's cousin Niamh French, who'd handled the Whyte case, was absorbed in her work on the computer, and hadn't been listening. But now she took off her headset, and pushed her chair back as she stood up. The other three turned to look at her—and saw the video display for the first time. They tensed, staring at the young man who sat there, strapped securely to the chair. They couldn't hear his screaming—they weren't wearing the headset—but they could see how his face contorted in trauma and desperation.

"The people we're dealing with don't really take prisoners," Niamh announced to the others, as their glances turned to her questioningly. "I looked through the entire security camera feed and found only two. This... man? boy? and a young adult. A girl." She paused and glanced at the current display. "This guy looks like he's one of them—turned traitor, or something of the sort."

"That could be helpful to us," Darek noted thoughtfully. He stared hard at the struggling form in the chair. Something about the boy was familiar, but Darek couldn't quite tell what it was.

"And here's the other one." Niamh switched screens to show a video of a young lady, around nineteen. She was sitting on a bench in a small, bare room, facing what was probably the door. Her right arm was in a sling, and she sat there, staring pensively up at the camera. "I know her," Niamh added. "Nina Marwick, paramedic."

"I've met her," Darek put in. "She's a smart girl. What's she doing in there?"

"Probably your description of 'smart girl' answers that question," Joyce replied humorlessly. "I think the real question is: How is she still alive?"

Erin shrugged. "Maybe she knows something?"

Niamh glanced sharply at her younger cousin, her face breaking into a warm smile of approval. "You're probably right!"

Erin blushed. "Okay, then, but what could she know?"

Joyce made an impatient gesture. "Whatever she knows, the Encephalon people obviously don't know it, and it's important, or they wouldn't be keeping her. We can work off that. This doesn't really change the plan, does it?" she asked, glancing at Darek, who was the senior officer present.

He shook his head. "No. In fact it makes things better for us. Where are they keeping these prisoners?"

* * *

It was almost twenty-four hours later when the security alarms went off at Encephalon Center 01, Annapolis, Maryland. There had been a breach.

"Two unidentified near Exit 8," a monotone speaker insisted repeatedly. "Two unidentified near Exit 8. Emergency lockdown initiated."

Trinity had been giving Lyndon a report, but when she heard the alert, she told him goodbye. "Something's happening, Dad," she said. "I'll call you back when it's over." Then she hung up and zipped up her bulletproof jacket, strapped on her night vision goggles, and headed out of her office into the corridor.

Out there, everything seemed normal at first glance. But that was one of the disadvantages of having a huge underground base with dozens of exits.

A sensor could be tripped a kilometer away, and the whole place would lock down. Trinity would've ignored the breach, if her office—and the main laboratory area—hadn't been on the same side of the building as Exit 8. Exit 8 was the gun shop, and Trinity was a few floors below that.

In the corridor, she could hear Conner Whyte yelling from a few rooms away. She winced. Every time she left her office she could hear him. Always screaming. It was getting on her nerves. And she realized he was screaming as loudly as he could, now, probably because he'd heard the alert as well.

Most likely he was trying to attract the attention of any possible rescuers. Trinity pushed aside the ridicule that sprang to her mind at the prospect of rescue, and frowned. "Never underestimate your enemy" was one of her favorite watchwords.

A Sensor soldier was hurrying by, intent on their own business, whatever it was, but Trinity called them out. "You," she said quickly, and they stopped, and turned. "Go shut him up, will you?"

The girl soldier saluted, her hand trembling nervously, and rushed to carry out the order. Trinity headed for the elevator at the end of the hall, meanwhile radioing her officers to tell her what was going on. She wasn't getting much of an answer, so she got into the elevator and went up.

thirty-five

Conner heard the door behind him open, and he yelled even louder, hoping someone might hear him. The door closed, and he braced himself for some retribution. He knew from experience that the people who worked in Encephalon could get touchy about too much noise, especially during a security breach. But instead, he heard a calm, reassuring voice.

"Keep screaming."

He twisted his head around as far as he could, but in vain.

The Violet Army officer came around the chair, holding her gun at the ready, and he could see the badge on her uniform—what was supposed to be a circle of nerve axons—that told him she was a Sensor, a Violet Army soldier without the superhuman injection. She looked about twenty-four, with dark brown, almost black hair, and olive skin. She wore the entire uniform, but the visor of the helmet was up, and he could hear and see her clearly. To his utter surprise, she turned her back to the camera, facing him, and smiled slightly.

But then she frowned.

"I said keep screaming," she ordered curtly, holding her gun up in clear view of the camera—aiming directly at Conner. The sixteen-year-old shut his eyes tight—and screamed.

The next instant, the Sensor fired—Conner opened his eyes and stared in shock at the officer, who was turning around from shooting at the camera. There was just a hole in the corner, with a mess of wires, to show where the device had once been.

He glanced back at the woman, who was looking hard at him. "Who are you?" she asked him briefly.

Conner blinked in surprise. He could hardly believe what he was seeing.

"Conner Whyte," he replied quietly, and his hoarse, parched voice sounded strange in his ears. "Aka Trooper A1. Who are you?"

"Joyce Liszt, U.S.A. Marine paratrooper," Joyce told him, still watching the boy carefully. "Now look. We haven't got a lot of time, so we can save stories for later. I don't really care why you're here, all I need to know is whose side you're on."

"Are you with Trinity?" Conner asked, though he already knew the answer.

A look of disgust crossed Joyce's face. "Ryder? Are you kidding me?"

"Then I'm with you," Conner acquiesced, meeting her gaze so she could see he was telling the truth. "You said U.S.A.?"

"Yeah. We're gonna wipe out these Encephalon people, and we're counting on you to help us. But before I get you out of that chair, I need to know you're actually gonna help us," Joyce finished. She locked eyes with Conner.

"I'll help you," he returned swiftly. "I'll help you. I have a few debts around here to return," he added softly, in a voice full of mixed hope and fury. His eyes burned like a flame rekindled.

"No doubt you do," Joyce agreed, going around to the back of the chair. "Do you know how this thing works?"

"There's some sort of button back there that releases the entire thing, I don't know quite what it looks like but—" Conner broke off as there was a click and the straps released. For a second it didn't register, but then he got up. He stood there, in front of the chair, letting his blood flow. He had never felt so cramped. Where the straps had been, he was just numb, and there were red blisters from his continuous fight against them. Conner stretched, trying to get some of his former energy back. Then a sharp sting in his hand reminded him he was still connected to the IV machine.

Joyce had already noticed it. "You've got a needle in your hand," she remarked, but Conner had already clenched his teeth and torn the tape off and the IV needle with it. He left it where it was, swinging uselessly from the machine. A crimson blob formed on his wrist where the needle had been, but he ignored it.

"How long have I been in here?" he asked the paratrooper, who was busy adjusting something around the collar of her Violet Army suit.

She looked up briefly. "You can answer that better than I can," she retorted, then turned her attention back to whatever she was doing. A moment later, seemingly, she'd finished.

Conner was watching her. "What's the plan?"

"What's the plan?" Joyce repeated absently. "Break you and the other kid out, make as big a mess as we can manage, and then clear out of here," she listed. "There are three with me. Let's go meet them." She paused with her hand on the doorknob, glancing at the Inter helmet sitting on the small counter against the wall. "Is that yours?"

Conner nodded, and picked it up. "I think so," he replied, his voice getting muffled by the helmet halfway through the sentence.

Joyce grinned. "Let's go, then."

* * *

Nina didn't look up as the door opened. She was too busy slouching and staring thoughtfully at the floor tiles, and besides she didn't really want to acknowledge her visitor's presence. From the steady click-click of Violet Army boot heels, she already knew exactly who it was.

"Hey," the visitor spoke finally, standing directly in front of Nina. "Still hanging in there?"

"Hey," Nina replied, deigning to lift her head from her uninjured arm and look up at the woman. She dropped her hand in her lap, and sat up, leaning against the wall. "Mhmm. Still alive. Is that bad or good?"

"Good," Reina Patterson replied carefully, her mouth set in a hard line. "Now, do you remember what I told you last time?"

"Remind me," Nina shrugged, smiling grimly.

"If you insist," returned the Reflex officer. Her eyes narrowed as Nina continued to grin defiantly. "We Encephalon need to know some things, and you're going to tell us. As I told you yesterday, after today we will find another way to make you talk, unless you make things easier for us and yourself by simply talking. Is that clear?"

"I guess," Nina muttered.

"Excellent. Then we can begin. Who was the fourth and unidentifi—" Reina's voice broke off as both of them heard the emergency alert blaring from the hall. Nina looked keenly interested, and Reina wheeled around, listening intently. She scowled deeply as she heard the words, "Exit 8."

"I'll be back," Reina promised, swinging the door open with an angry gesture. It swung closed on its own. Nina could hear the click as Reina locked it from the other side, and then she could hear her footsteps as she marched away. The clacks gradually grew more and more faint, till she couldn't hear them anymore. But now the corridor was full of noises from other people, as well as various machines beeping, as the entire place locked down. Nina waited until everything was quiet.

But then she sprang up, and hurried across the small room to the door, pushing against it lightly. Her forehead had broken out in cold sweat as Reina left, but now extreme relief crossed her face as the door opened. Nina had not let the day before go to waste, but instead she had been figuring out how the door's unique lock worked, and trying to sabotage it. Now she knew she had succeeded.

Stepping out into the hall, she glanced both ways down it to make sure that no one was there. Good; it was empty, as she'd hoped.

The young paramedic jogged down the hall towards the elevator, trying to make as little noise as she could in her light sneakers. To her great dismay, the elevator was already in use; the signals told her it was coming down, to floor three. She glanced at the number above the heavy elevator door.

thirty-six

Nina waited in the corner next to the elevator, little dreaming that Conner Whyte had done the same thing only a few months before. Her hands grew wet and clammy with the suspense. She could hear her heart pounding—*lub dub, lub dub,* her paramedic training subconsciously reminded her. She forced herself to take a deep breath to try and steady her nerves.

Ping. The elevator doors slid open, and she braced herself to tackle whoever might come out. She saw a shoe—and before her mind could register that it wasn't a Violet Army shoe, she'd already jumped. The newcomer shouted in surprise, as did Nina when she realized who it was. The paramedic scrambled away, literally breathing apologies. It was her friend Niamh French.

"Sorry, sorry, sorry!" Nina panted, leaning against the wall, gently repositioning her sling with her left hand.

Niamh stood up, looking bewildered. "O—kay?"

"Any other ambushers?" Erin asked cautiously from the elevator.

Nina's face was literally all red. "No, no, it's just me, I'm sorry. I didn't know you guys were—"

"It's fine, we can talk later," Niamh interrupted. "At least you're already out, which saves us some time. Let's get out of here," she added, stepping back into the elevator.

Nina followed her, glancing at Erin. "I didn't know you had a sister," she told Niamh in surprise, as the older police officer sent the elevator up to Level 1. The elevator room jolted into action, rising slowly. Niamh locked the doors, and shoved her sleeve up a bit, so she could read her watch.

"Cousin, actually," Erin interposed. She stuck out her hand, and took Nina's left. "Erin French, U.S. Marine. Nice to meet you."

"Nina Marwick," Nina introduced herself, her face breaking into a smile. "Nice to meet you, too."

"Let's review the plan," Niamh broke in, still gazing at her watch. With her other hand, she pulled her gun out of her belt. Erin did the same. "We have five minutes till we can expect Joyce and the other guy," Niamh told her friend and cousin. "We have to hold the elevator till then, and then we have to cover them."

"Other guy?" Nina questioned.

"Some kid that they've got in a chair in a room like yours," Niamh told her quietly. "Joyce Liszt is getting him out. They're going to smash up the laboratory, take another elevator to Level 1, run over here—probably under fire—and then we'll all head to ground level together. If we survive," she added doubtfully.

"Who's Joyce Liszt?" Nina wanted to know.

"A paratrooper like me," Erin replied, flushing slightly.

Nina grinned. "Okay. And the kid—?"

"We don't know," Niamh cut in.

Nina shrugged. "Okay. So do we just wait here for the next five minutes?" she added as the elevator dinged, announcing that they'd arrived.

Niamh nodded, making sure that the light next to *Doors Locked* was still glowing. She stepped away from the elevator door, in the corner of the elevator next to it, and motioned for Erin and Nina to do the same on the other side. "It's safer," she pointed out softly.

Nobody wanted to talk from that point on, and the seconds ticked away. Erin got out her second gun and handed it to Nina, who held it in her trembling left hand. The minutes dragged by, until finally Niamh reached for the door button, pressing it firmly. The elevator doors slid open, and the three young women could hear plainly what they had heard faintly a few seconds before.

The hallway was a scene of chaos. At least three people were yelling. Guns were going off into the ceiling; as the doors finished opening, Nina could hear one clear, loud voice shouting to them. "Heya Frenchies! We're coming!"

She could assume it was Joyce Liszt. A bullet came flying in between the doors, thudding into the back wall of the elevator. Niamh stuck her head out for a brief instant, took aim, and shot back. Someone in the hallway screamed. Niamh bit her lip and reloaded.

Next to Nina, Erin was doing the same thing, and Nina was trying to brace herself. She did in fact manage to pop her head out for a moment to try and see what was going on. She could seethe other paratrooper—Joyce Liszt—fighting her way out with the "kid"—

"It's Conner!" Nina exclaimed in surprise. Just when Conner and Joyce burst into the elevator, panting. A few shots followed them in, but they'd already crowded to the sides, and Joyce slammed her finger down on the doors button. Ever so slowly, the doors closed—Joyce and Niamh risked a few more shots. The heavy doors slid together with a dull thud, and Niamh sent them up to Level 0.

Nina glanced over at Conner. He was breathing heavily, and his visor was all fogged up. He pushed it up with a hand—it was smeared with red. He glanced at Nina, and she stared back. She could remember when he had been at least a foot shorter than her. But now, here he was, looking down from at least three inches above the tall, older paramedic.

"Nina?" he asked softly, pulling on thick combat gloves from his belt. Then he wiped off his helmet visor. But he was looking at Nina the entire time. "Nina Marwick?"

"You remember now?" Nina returned, a bit apprehensively.

The young soldier nodded. "What happened to Moira?"

"They said she got shot—" Nina began, but the conversation was interrupted by a jolt that shook the entire elevator.

The room stopped moving; an alarm on the ceiling went off, flashing red. Then the lights went out, and all that they had to see by was the eerie red light that played over the walls and floor of the elevator. Nina heard a click as Conner pulled his helmet visor back into place.

"What's going on?" she asked, feeling horribly uninformed.

"Stand back, everyone," Conner warned. In the faint red light,

Nina watched as Joyce, Niamh, and Erin backed away from the elevator door, arranging themselves against the back wall. The paramedic did the same.

Conner slammed his shoulder into the seam where the two doors met; the room shuddered, and Nina almost saw the doors shake momentarily. He did it again, with no real results, then yelled angrily and punched the control panel.

Something sparked; the alert light went off completely, and they were left in utter darkness. But the doors started to jerk open. Nina could see that the elevator hadn't completely made it up to ground level; there was an opening at the top, about two feet high, but from then on down was a bare concrete wall. Light poured in through the opening, and Conner jumped up, gripping the edge of the floor and pulling himself up with unbelievable strength.

He started laughing uncontrollably, in his hoarse, changing boy's voice, a sound Nina had never heard the likes of before. He couldn't stop laughing.

"Of all places!" Nina heard Conner shout through his helmet. "The hotel! I remember this lobby!"

He disappeared through the aperture, and Niamh shouted after him to help them get out, muttering something under her breath about kids.

Presently a chair came through; Joyce managed to grab it just in time. Above them it sounded like a war was breaking out. Shots were fired; someone was urgently radioing the Encephalon leader, calling for immediate reinforcements.

Joyce was the first to use the chair to scramble out of the elevator; then came Niamh, Erin, and finally Nina. The paramedic looked around for an instant before Erin shouted something unintelligible over the noise and grabbed Nina, dragging her behind a heavy desk.

thirty-seven

Nina looked around quickly, trying to take in her new surroundings. They were in the lobby of a local Annapolis hotel that she'd seen before—the elevator was the one that had always had the "Out of Order" sign taped to it for as long as she could remember.

The lobby was a mess. It had been deserted by all but a few Violet Army guards during the occupation, guards who were now amazed to find an infuriated, berserk sixteen-year-old Inter emerging from the elevator and rampaging as he went, covered by fire from three uniformed soldiers who obviously knew what they were doing as they coolly picked their targets, one by one.

"For Moira!" Conner yelled, charging the last remaining Reflex recklessly, the one who'd been calling for help. He threw him out the big front hotel window with a powerful twist. The officer landed in the street, surrounded by shattered glass. Conner leapt out the window after him, shouting for the others to follow. Joyce was already up and going, with Niamh and Erin following her example. They had to get out and as far away as possible before reinforcements arrived.

Erin glanced back at Nina, who was still getting to her feet. It was tricky with only one usable hand. "You okay?" the young paratrooper asked her, noting her new friend's whitish face.

"Yeah, I'm fine," Nina nodded quickly, running after Conner, Joyce, and Niamh.

They stood in the street, the five of them. No one was there. But then a truck came speeding up, stopping just in front of them. Darek looked out through the window.

"Get in!" he yelled, but he needn't have. Niamh was already yanking the passenger door open. They could hear the first sounds of pursuit.

Conner saw at a glance that there were only five seats total, and headed for the truck bed. "I'll cover our getaway," he shouted as the girls packed into the car. Nina found herself sandwiched between Joyce and Erin. She looked around for a buckle, but the paratroopers didn't appear too concerned at all, and Darek slammed his foot down on the pedal, sending the car flying ahead. Nina gave up on buckling her seat belt.

"How's it going, Miss Marwick?" Darek asked casually, glancing momentarily at the rearview mirror.

"I'm okay," Nina panted. Erin gave her a thumbs-up.

Conner was banging on the back window of the truck, and now Joyce twisted around to open it. "They've got motorcyclists after us," the boy reported breathlessly. "Their design. Faster than—" he glanced at Darek's speedometer— "Faster than one hundred miles per hour," he finished.

Darek gritted his teeth, pressing down harder while skillfully maneuvering the truck through the city's intersections. If there had been traffic that day, they would have crashed twenty times already. "I don't think we can go much faster!" he returned.

Conner had already gathered as much, and he sat up in the back, somehow positioning himself so that he wouldn't fall off at the terrific speed they were going. He took aim and shot at the motorcyclist in the lead, but right as he pulled the trigger the truck went over a pothole and his shot went wide.

Muttering, he tried again, this time with better luck. He hit the cyclist's tire, sending the motorcycle flying—the rider had been going so fast that they were thrown off it into the air, with a scream that ended horribly abruptly when they hit a wall. Nina cringed.

Suddenly the truck tires squealed, and the truck went a few more feet before spinning around dizzyingly. Finally it stopped, aided by smashing into a street lamp post. Nina felt like she was going to throw up.

"Puncture," Conner reported unnecessarily.

"Oh joy," Joyce yelled angrily, ducking instinctively as a bullet whizzed past her through the back window and then through the front.

"What now?" Erin asked tentatively. "Joyce, what do we d—"

"We can't run anymore," Darek interrupted calmly. "We just have to face them now. Everybody got a gun?"

"Yeah," Niamh replied, craning her neck to look around.

"Then we'll take as many as we can with us," Darek decided grimly. "Good luck, everyone."

"Nina, I need to know," came Conner's urgent voice from the very back of the truck. "Is Moira alive or dead?"

"Conner, I don't know!" Nina shouted exasperatedly. "They told me she was dead!"

"Conner?" Darek asked from the front seat. He was the only one who hadn't yet been introduced to the latest addition to their small group which, it now seemed, was not going to last much longer.

"Conner Whyte," Joyce supplied quietly.

"Wait, that kid who got murdered? The one I smashed my hand going after his killer?" Darek sounded exhausted. "You gotta be kidding me. Well, nice to meet you, Conner."

"Is Moira alive or dead!" Conner screamed, sounding like how he'd sounded only half an hour before. He risked a shot at the fast approaching Violet Army vehicles.

"Who's Moira, if I may ask?" Joyce asked dryly.

"His twin s—" Nina began, but she was interrupted by sudden rapid fire from above. The sound was deafening.

Nina, Joyce, Darek, Niamh, and Erin all turned to look behind them. Conner was staring up at the sky.

"Dendrites," he announced somberly for their benefit. "But they aren't targeting us, they're targeting—"

He didn't finish the sentence. He didn't have to. They could all see it for themselves as a veritable line of drones flew directly in the path of the Violet Army, hovered there an instant, and then shot, all at the same time, causing total chaos in the Violet Army ranks. The drones bounced around wildly, then got into formation again and shot once more.

In a few seconds, it was all over. The six in the truck realized in the silence that followed that they'd been holding their breaths.

"Who did that?" Joyce breathed. "Or was it some crazy programming error?"

"It wasn't an error," Conner gave his opinion, hopping out of the back of the truck. "They don't have programming errors."

He landed easily on the pavement beside the vehicle as the drones sped upward into the sky and then disappeared among the gray winter-day clouds.

The young soldier looked around briefly. "I think we have allies."

"Yeah, here they are," Niamh agreed, stepping out of the passenger seat. She pointed down the opposite street, where she could see some dark-dressed people approaching. They were running. She could make out the forms of three people in front, all of various heights, and then she thought she could see another person behind them, running slowly but surely.

Darek, Erin, Nina, and Joyce joined her outside the truck.

They all stood against it, facing the four newcomers. The sun was in their eyes.

"Are they friends or are they ene—" Conner began, tilting his helmet visor to block the sun out of his face. He could see more clearly now, and his question was cut short as the fourth person sprinted, overtaking and passing the other three, and came pounding down the final stretch of about a kilometer's distance.

He recognized the person.

He froze, and stared, momentarily paralyzed.

But then he found himself running, running faster than he'd ever run before, with the icy wind in his face and a lump in his throat.

She saw him, and started running faster, as well. They slammed into each other, but neither cared. Conner found himself crying as they hugged so hard he was afraid his ribs would crack. Then they were both crying, and laughing, and talking all at once. He was sobbing like a baby, but smiling as if his face would fall off. He had never dreamed he would hug his older sister like this, him taller and stronger now in ways he had never thought possible, but here he was, hugging her as if she'd come back to life—which, in his view, she had.

"Moira!" he cried, everything he'd felt in the last four days coming out in the word, relieving his chest of an awful weight. And he could breathe again.

"Conner!" Moira was laughing, and crying, but also shoving her twin brother away. "Stop! You're going to squeeze me to death!"

"Moira! I thought you were dead!" he whispered, immediately loosening his deadly bear hug.

"I never thought you were dead," she returned softly. She finally managed to stand back and then looked at him, and hugged him again. "You're so tall!"

He finally realized something. She was wearing his coat, his favorite blue one, and it looked slightly too small for her, but it still triggered all sorts of memories of playing in the snow together with his sister. "Hey," he managed to choke out. "That's my coat."

She laughed, eyeing him thoughtfully. "I think you might've grown out of it."

thirty-eight

Around them, introductions were being made. Conner straightened suddenly when he heard his name being repeated, and he and Moira looked up.

He recognized Jack and Cloe, of course, but he couldn't put a name to the tall, energetic Italian who was talking—and quite animatedly too—with Darek and Niamh. "Who's that?" he asked Moira quietly.

Moira glanced over, and laughed. "That's Giulia Pervitto. You remember the Italian waitress who served us at the restaurant some months ago? With the cousins? Lila's birthday party?"

Conner was shocked to find that he actually remembered. He smiled. It was such a great feeling—having memories.

"Yeah, I remember."

Moira looked hard at him, and the two identical pairs of deep, blue eyes met. Then she was smiling too. "Well, I'm glad you remember."

They both turned as Joyce snapped her fingers, looking directly at Conner. "Conner Whyte?" she asked, seeming preoccupied. "I think we need some introductions." She pointed half-heartedly at Giulia, Darek, and Niamh. "I believe those three know each other, but—but—" She broke off. Moira started laughing again. Giulia's hand gestures were going double dutch.

"Yeah, um, sure," Conner nodded, suddenly realizing his eyes were still full of tears. He brushed his arm across his face awkwardly. "This is my twin sister, M—"

"Moira Whyte," Moira interposed, too used to introducing herself and her twin instead of the other way around. "And you are—?"

"Joyce Liszt, U.S.A. Marine paratrooper," Joyce returned. Moira's face broke into a giant grin. "Oh cool!"

"That's Erin," Joyce gestured towards her friend, who was standing shyly on the sidelines.

"And the Italian is Giulia, and those are Jack and Cloe," Moira finished, pointing. Conner looked at Jack, to find that his former best friend had already been looking at him.

They looked at each other for a moment, then Conner looked down at the ground. He was already feeling overwhelmed, and now he wondered what Jack was thinking. He had seen the entire thing; Conner shuddered just remembering it. But Moira had forgiven him, so maybe Jack would too. Or had she?

He glanced at his twin again, apprehensively this time. But she was still smiling brightly at him. Again he felt overwhelmed.

Everything was so different. This felt so strange. He had his memories, but they weren't like this.

Suddenly something struck him. "Moira, where's Mom? And Dad?"

Moira's face fell. "Mom's in the hospital, and—"

"*Attenzione!*" Giulia interrupted. "We can't stay here forever, peoples. Let's go!"

Moira nodded, and followed the adults at a steady pace down the street over to a large moving van. Conner followed silently. But then he felt someone slap his back, hard, and he wheeled around to see Jack.

"Hey." The older boy's face was blank.

"Hey," Conner returned, meeting his friend's gaze levelly.

Slowly Jack smiled. "You done shooting people, bro?"

"I've reformed." Conner smiled back. "You done jumping on people?"

Jack's eyebrows shot up. "I'll consider that one. But the real question is—"

"Oh, cut it out, Jack," Nina's voice broke in. She was sounding impatient. "Are we getting into that van?" The paramedic pointed over to where Giulia was hopping in the driver's seat of a twelve-passenger van.

Jack nodded. "Yeah. How many of us are there?" He did a quick count. "Nine, ten... Yeah. We'll just fit. Maybe we'll have to squeeze, but we'll fit."

"Why would we have to squeeze?" Conner wondered aloud, glancing at the van. It looked big enough to him.

Jack scoffed. "Because that twin sister of yours has got the back row filled with her hacking equipment, that's why!"

Conner was slightly surprised to hear his sister affiliated with hacking, but it wasn't that much of a shock. "Okay, then," he acquiesced, looking down at his friend. "You can sit on my lap," he offered.

The older, yet much shorter, boy glared. "Maybe if you wanna—"

"Hey, we're leaving!" Cloe waved wildly from the door of the van. They heard the engines start. Conner and Jack suddenly realized everyone else was inside, and they took off at a run for the doors. Conner swung himself in efficiently after Jack, just as Giulia pushed hard on the pedal and the van lurched forward. After the first breathless moment of sickening inertia, Conner finished stepping in, and grabbed the handhold at the roof, slamming the door shut after him.

Cloe was in the seat next to the door, and she glanced up at him briefly. "Moira's in the back," she pointed, buckling her seat belt.

Conner nodded, and carefully made his way to the back of the van, a tedious process. But when he did get there, Moira had a seat cleared off for him. He sat down—and she promptly deposited a boxful of Violet Army drones on his lap, ignoring his groan of protest.

"Shh," she warned, turning on the big screen that was attached to the back of the seat in front of her. After a few seconds, the display came on. Conner gawked. It was an aerial view of the van, that followed them as they drove.

"Drones," Moira answered his question before he asked it. "I borrowed around fifty from your overstocked Violet Army supplies. You don't mind, do you?"

"I—" Conner began to stammer, before he realized she was grinning like an idiot. "Not at all," he finished lamely. "How's that thing powered?"

"We tapped into your electricity source as well," Moira returned, still grinning. "In fact we've got a lot of stuff going on from you Enci people. Like it?"

"H—how?" was all he could manage, tongue-tied at his twin's prowess for not the first time in his life. He had to smile to himself. He might be bigger and stronger now, but no matter what he did he'd never outwit his sister!

Her smile widened. "Well, after you disappeared," she began accusingly, "I decided to up my computer science grade, that's all. This is why you stare at computer screens all day. So, like it?"

"Moira," he told her seriously, "I really need an update. And can we start with the question are you really and truly okay after falling off that roof after I—" He choked, and couldn't continue.

Moira shrugged uneasily. "I'm not going to compliment you on your aim, if that's what you're going for. But really, that Giulia Pervitto is amazing. I can't understand why she went into the waitress business at all. She's been on the run for months. I don't know the entire story, but—"

"I do," Conner interrupted. "Can we skip to the next part of it, please?"

Moira laughed. "Okay. Well, she found me, and patched me up, and we found Cloe and Jack after that, a couple of days ago. To be honest, Giulia isn't that bad at hacking, either. She already had a few things set up here." Moira paused, and glanced around the back row of four seats, most of which were completely enshrouded in boxes of computer supplies. "But I already knew a lot about the Enci, and I took it from there."

Moira took a deep breath, hoping she wasn't sounding too prideful. "I think the Dendrites have a production flaw—if you get water into their insides, they burn a fuse, and you can replace it—and then program them to do whatever you like." She grinned. "As you saw a few minutes ago."

"That was really amazing," Conner complimented her, smiling. "We thought we were goners."

Moira giggled. "I didn't even know you were there. Giulia and I were just running them over the city, and then we saw trouble, and Giulia was like, '*Stupidos*!' So we came to the rescue. It was fun actually," she added, chuckling.

Conner grinned. "Lucky for us. Who's the policeman? Or do you not know?"

"Oh, Darek?" Moira lifted her head for a moment to listen to the voices up front. "He was on your case when you went missing. And then he smashed his hand so they had to let him go—which was why he wasn't on the Violet Army execution list, I guess. So he's survived. And Niamh actually quit because she was going to be teaching for a better salary, so that's why she's here too."

"Oh," Conner breathed, taking in the information. "So what are you guys up to?" he asked then.

"Us?" Moira shrugged. "Really, before we jumped in to save you guys' lives, we were just trying to stay hidden and get information to the U.S. Army. But now that we're probably gonna have the entire Violet Army down on us, we're going to have to change tactics. I bet there's going to be a meeting later."

thirty-nine

Moira was right, as her twin found out some hours later. They'd gotten to Giulia's current hideout—a car storage garage that she claimed she would turn into a restaurant of her own one fine day—just after dark, and everyone had opted to begin the night with a few hours' rest.

Conner, Darek, and Jack shared a small room. The exhausted police officer and Jack fell asleep almost right away, but Conner had some trouble following their example. He lay awake some time, thinking.

The choice of base really was amazing. Conner had passed it half a dozen times on patrol routes and never once had he suspected a thing. He remembered that now and hoped the rest of the Violet Army would make the same mistake.

He hadn't really wanted to lie down at first, but now that he had, he realized he was somewhat tired. After all, it had been one of the most climactic days of his life thus far.

Now that everything was peaceful, for the time being, he could hear Moira talking faintly from the other room, but not who she was talking to. He wondered, and decided it was probably Nina.

Conner smiled to himself. It was so good to hear his sister's voice again.

* * *

And now they were getting ready for a meeting. Conner had changed out of his Inter suit into normal, casual clothing and was waiting for the others in the designated "meeting room"—a dimly lit, partitioned section of the garage. There was a chalkboard, with a few dilapidated pieces of chalk on it, standing just below the one window. Cobwebs decorated the walls; a few rickety chairs stood around.

Conner didn't sit down. He glanced at the digital clock on the wall; it read 5:04 AM. He wondered if it told the correct time. But as there wasn't any real light shining through the dusty window, he assumed it was correct.

He heard voices, and footsteps, and then some of the others showed up: Moira, Darek, and the three Marwicks. He was surprised to see that Moira and Cloe were carrying steaming paper cups, one in each hand. Cloe gave hers to Darek and Nina; Moira, to Jack and her twin. The two girls turned to get more for themselves, but Conner's voice stopped Moira. He was looking into his cup.

"Hot chocolate?" he asked Moira incredulously.

Moira nodded cheerfully. "Mhmm. We discovered that if you boil hot water it kills the LVED, or whatever. And boiling water is only one step away from hot chocolate," she finished, grinning.

"Oh," Conner breathed, lifting his cup to his nose and sniffing the rich, warm, chocolaty aroma. He let it fill his lungs, wondering when was the last time he had smelled something this nice. Moira laughed and darted out.

She was back a few seconds later, followed by Giulia, Niamh, Erin, and Joyce. Nina, Moira, and Cloe ended up being the ones to get seats; the others didn't really seem to care, like Conner. He leaned against the wall behind Moira's chair, watching as the others chose places around the room; suddenly he realized Giulia was looking right at him. With her free hand—the other held her cup of hot chocolate—she pointed vehemently at the teenager.

"You!" she shouted accusingly, and everyone glanced up. "You, there!"

Conner stared back. "Yes?" he asked calmly.

"You gave me a real bad five minutes." Giulia's pointing finger moved so fast he couldn't keep track of it. "You were that soldier in the sign-up whatever room, weren't you!"

"I was," Conner choked out, feeling desperately embarrassed.

"And you chased me out the window! I could have ended up like your sister here if there hadn't been a big van below!" Giulia glanced at Moira for an instant, seemingly not realizing that the girl would have seemed perfectly fine if she hadn't been wearing a brace, which actually didn't bother Moira at all.

"Sorry," Conner returned, hoping she wouldn't go on. Everyone was staring at him now, except Moira. He could see her shoulders shaking as she laughed silently, and he had to force himself not to grin. Grinning would be the worst thing to do while apologizing for shooting at someone and chasing them out of a window.

"Your name is Trooper," Giulia continued, after a moment's recollection. "Trooper! Of all the names—!"

"Actually, it's Conner," Moira intervened in her twin's defense. Conner managed a weak, half-smile.

"Trooper," Giulia went on obliviously. "It sounds like—"

"My name is Conner," Conner interrupted himself this time. "And I'm sorry. I wasn't quite myself—"

He stopped excusing himself when Giulia smiled, a big, vibrant smile that assured him he was fine. But the next instant, the former waitress scowled, and Conner bit his lip.

"I can forgive you everything but the name Trooper," she decided. "Anything else would've been fine, but to hear a 'Trooper' ordered to shoot you—"

"How about 'A1-93VA'?" Jack asked pensively.

Conner glared at him. "A1-93VA" was the number on his uniform.

"Huh?" Giulia turned her attention to the eighteen-year-old Marwick boy.

"What if you heard an 'A1-93VA' ordered to shoot you?" Jack repeated patiently.

"Jack, shut up," Nina hissed from across the room.

Giulia apparently decided Jack's question wasn't worth answering, or else she had short-term memory, because now she glanced over at the other adults, Joyce, Darek, Erin, and Niamh, who were looking thoroughly bored, but too polite to say so. "So!" the Italian began. "This is a planning meeting, after all. Who'll begin?" She glanced pointedly at Darek, and went on to answer her own question. "I'll bet you already have a plan?"

Darek cleared his throat. "Yes, I believe we do, but we'll have to make some minor changes."

Giulia shrugged. "Fire away. And feel free to use the chalkboard, if you need it."

The half-hour that followed was a torturous one for Conner. Darek very often turned to the teenager, asking for comments from the one person there who knew the Violet Army defenses in and out. Conner in turn found himself either nodding, or shaking his head and explain why something would not work. Then he would have to think of a workaround. Altogether, it was a very time-consuming process, but finally Darek came to what he called the culmination of the entire plan—if it failed, everything failed.

"Niamh and Joyce discovered that the power source that connects to all the Violet Army combat suits is here." He tapped a portion of the blackboard with his index finger. "If we cut that source, not only will their communication, etc. stop working, their suits will also freeze, and they won't be able to move. This is because—"

"The Myelin gel freezes instantly," Conner interjected. "It isn't quite a power source that keeps it liquid, though. To prevent the suits being easily replicated, the suit's built-in energy system that keeps the Myelin at room temperature and runs the other apparati is set to a certain wavelength. This radio signal is the same for all the suits, and is generated by the Schwann, which is located inside Encephalon. If we can take out the Schwann, we can take all the Inters, Sensors, Reflex, Motors—you name it."

"What's the Myelin for, anyway?" Moira muttered.

Conner grinned. "Biology class should've given you a hint," he noted. "The Myelin is a substance the Enci invented, like the G-fiber. The G-fiber is the outer layer of the typical Violet Army suit, and it's bulletproof and puncture-proof, which is a good thing, because between it and another layer of G-fiber is the Myelin gel, which absorbs the shock. By the way, Myelin gel is extremely dangerous, I've heard, and if there's a spill—" He grimaced. "But that's what the G-fiber is there for, right?"

Giulia hated long speeches; she cleared her throat meaningfully. "So if we blow up that S-whatever machine, the Violets go BOOM!—and we've won?"

"Oh, no, no," Conner hastened to correct himself. "They just can't move, and if they're in there too long, they may literally freeze."

"We should figure out a way to contain them before we try this," Darek decided, and made a note accordingly.

"Who's gonna take out the Schwann?" Jack wondered aloud. "I would imagine it'd be hard to get to. I mean, I wouldn't leave the key to your army sitting on the windowsill—"

"I'll do it," Joyce and Conner both interrupted at the same time. They glanced at each other in surprise.

"I will," Joyce iterated firmly. "I owe it to America."

Conner stared at her rather. "I mean, believe me when I say *I'm* the only one who *can* do it..."

"Why?" Joyce asked point-blank.

Conner shrugged. "Well, have you had a T4 injection?" he returned softly. "No, but I have. And I know Encephalon like the back of my hand. Trust me."

"But a T4 injection alone won't get you there and back safely," Moira interposed. "What are you going to do there?"

The two pairs of dark blue eyes met.

"I'll wear my suit," Conner replied. "You'll get me out of there before I freeze to death, right?"

"Yeah, we'll get you out of there in time," Darek answered for Moira, and for all of them as well. "So that's decided?"

"Yes," Conner nodded emphatically. Moira shook her head and mouthed *No* silently, but Darek didn't see her.

"I guess," Joyce muttered reluctantly.

"Then we'll do that, then," Darek concluded. He set to erasing the chalkboard. "When do we put this plan into action?"

forty

"Maughan has no idea what happened to him. He just keeps saying that there are things that science can't explain. But I know, and the security camera feed agrees, that he is completely himself again."

Trinity paused, and listened to her father's instructions over the radio. Lyndon Arnnu was in Cincinnati, Ohio, finishing up there before moving on to his next destination. But now he wasn't so sure he should keep going, if Trinity was having trouble in Annapolis.

Trinity shook her head. "Oh, no, Dad! I can totally handle it. You're fine!"

"How do you know?" Lyndon asked her pointedly.

"Because A1 has that backup implant, remember? We have sound, and location, but no video. They were finishing their conference just before you called. They intend to attack Encephalon tonight." Trinity bit her lip.

"Then I'm coming back now." Lyndon's tones, even over the radio, were decisive.

"Dad—I thought about it. We can't both be in the same place. Attacking Encephalon is not their only plan—their main objective is the Schwann," Trinity revealed. "Second main objective is contacting the outside world through our Lens broadcasting network and telling them how to neutralize the LVED. But you have the Lens with you." She paused. "If it's not here, then they can only succeed with the Schwann—except they won't even succeed with that, of course. But you see what I mean, right?"

"Yeah. You want me to stay here, with the Lens. That's it?"

"Mhmm. I can handle things here." Trinity laughed. "There are only ten of them, after all. And it's all the people in the world who know enough about us to be a threat." She smiled grimly.

"Well then, we need to finish them off, for once and for all."

"I can do that," Trinity agreed.

"They can't be allowed to get away." Lyndon sounded urgent. "And we're taking no prisoners this time."

"Right," Trinity nodded. "I'll let them get pretty far with their plan. But once we have them all in the net—"

A quiet chuckle from her father. "Then we've won. I'm counting on you, Trinity."

"I'll win, Dad," the young adult assured him.

"Good. Signing off then. But how are you, Vi, personally?"

"I'm great, Dad." Trinity smiled. "I really am."

"That's good. I'll see you soon, Vi."

"See you soon, Dad." She hung up.

"I'll win," she repeated, to herself this time. But if anyone had been in the room, they would have heard the strange tone in her voice that made her not sound too sure.

The mood didn't stay. The next instant she leapt up from her desk, throwing on her jacket. It was time to see about Encephalon's defenses.

* * *

"I'm not feeling so sure about this anymore," Conner had to admit, tossing his helmet from hand to hand. He wasn't going to put it on until he was done talking and everything else was ready to go.

Moira laughed from where she was putting the finishing touches to a tracker in the motorcycle next to Conner. "What's so frightening about it?"

Conner shrugged uncomfortably. "Nothing really. Just riding a motorcycle at break-neck speed through the wall of a building and then going down a long flight of stairs with it, that's all." He pushed a strand of his longish light blond hair out of his face, and realized with a start that he was already sweating. He was more nervous than even *he* knew.

Moira looked up at him briefly, pushing her own, longer, light brown hair out of her face. "Well, that's what the G-fiber is for, isn't it?" she jibed.

Her face softened at the imploring look on his face. "Hey, I'm just kidding."

"You'll get me out of this as soon as you can, won't you?" Conner asked anxiously. He looked down at his Violet Army suit. "I may be an Inter but I can't stand up against freezing temperatures for too much longer than a normal person can."

"Yeah, we'll get you out," Jack assured him. The boy was standing nearby, as were most of the others, though Moira and Conner were the only ones really talking at the moment—except Jack. "Even if we have to use explosives," the teenager added darkly.

"Shut up," Moira warned her brother's friend.

"Is he ready to go?" Darek asked, walking over. He looked over the tall, muscular boy, and grinned at him.

Conner managed a weak smile. "Yeah. I'm ready to go."

With his sister, the police officer, and his friend watching him, he put one leg over the motorcycle, and then sat down. The motorcycle was one Joyce and he had managed to "borrow" from Encephalon supplies: a sleek, streamlined purple motorcycle capable of impossible speeds. It was just his size.

Conner took a deep breath, then slid his helmet over his head. There was the moment of blindness, and then he could see again, through the purple-tinted visor. He hoped it wouldn't fog up again.

He wrapped his hands around the motorcycle handles, and let his fingers relax. He had ridden one of these before. Maybe even the same one. There was no reason to be worried about anything, he reminded himself. They were literally designed for wartime use; he could go through a wall easily with it.

Moira was right. There was no reason he should fail, especially as Joyce had improved on his suit by adding a double collar for neck protection. The Encephalon knew nothing about the attack hovering over their heads. They were going to win.

And when they did, everything would go back to normal. They'd get him out of his frozen suit. And he and Moira could be twins again, and lead normal lives. Maybe their mother would get better. And hopefully their father was still alright, so far away in Washington.

He looked up. Ahead of him, Cloe was opening the heavy garage door. It was dusk outside, but there was still enough sunlight to color the pavement yellow. Now the door was completely open.

It was time to go.

Conner glanced at his twin sister. Moira smiled encouragingly. “Chin up, trooper, and let’s go crush this,” she told him.

A brief memory of a long-past volleyball game flitted through Conner’s head, and he smiled back. A real smile this time. It was more than enough for Moira, and her dark eyes lit up.

“We’ll win this time,” he muttered. “I promise.”

Then he flipped the switch. The motorcycle engine started up; a low, rumbling vibration filled the garage atmosphere. Cloe backed away from the door.

And the next instant Trooper A1 was on his way.

forty-one

"I like their spirit," Trinity commented, watching the video display on the huge screen in the monitoring room. She was standing behind the desk chair; in it sat a naïve female Inter.

"Who are they?" the young lady asked. She was probably twenty at the most—Trinity was younger than her, but Trinity was so much higher ranked that for the Inter it was like talking to someone older.

Trinity stared hard at the three forms walking directly towards the hidden, ground-view camera, with the black specks hovering dozens of feet in the air. "The one in the center is Moira Whyte," Trinity told her. "That's Giulia Pervitto, and that's either Erin or Niamh French." She squinted. "I can't quite tell."

"And those specks—those are Dendrites, yes?"

"Yes." Trinity paused. "Oh, that Whyte girl knows we're watching her. I guess this is her idea of an epic entrance."

"It's not that bad," the girl muttered.

Trinity allowed herself a grim smile of satisfaction. "Oh, I know. Maughan!" she called.

Her Head of Security came over quickly, taking in the scene on the screen instantly. "Do I wipe them out?" he demanded.

"How?" Trinity asked simply.

"With a Motor team, of course," Hilton returned, somewhat confused.

Trinity shook her head. "The Dendrites will wreak havoc. Don't waste our people on them now; wait. The Dendrites cannot help them inside," Trinity pointed out. "These three are the Lens team. They think it's in the broadcasting room. Take thirty Inters, and wait for them there—that's ten T4s to one normal human. You can't lose," she finished flatly. "Or you can have someone else do that, and instead take twenty to protect the lab from the cop's team."

"I'll do that." Hilton nodded. He turned, and marched out of the room, yelling to one of his coworkers through his helmet intercom. "Lafferty! Take your unit to the broadcasting room!"

"Will do," came the quick response.

"Good," Hilton replied, and cut the intercom. "Kids are worse than cops," he muttered to himself as he went to go pick up his own unit.

"What are you going to do, Trin?" the Inter wanted to know.

"Me?" Trinity smiled. "I'm going to wait, for now at least."

* * *

"I would've expected something by now," Moira was saying, frowning. "Surely they can see us here!"

"Maybe they're distracted," Niamh shrugged. "What time is Conner due again?"

Moira glanced at her watch. "Any minute now."

"Then we should just head in, right? Maybe he's early," Niamh decided.

Moira opened her mouth to disagree, but Giulia was all for it. "Right! *AVANTI!*" she shouted, starting to run. Moira sighed and tore after her as fast as she could with her back still in a brace from her fall.

"That wasn't the kind of heading in I meant," Niamh muttered, but she took off anyway.

* * *

"You ready to go, kid?" Darek asked, glancing at the nervous-looking teenager beside him.

Jack nodded tentatively. "Yeah. Yeah, I think," he managed, moving his gun from one hand to the other. Jack was no beginner at shooting, but when it came to something like this he just couldn't concentrate fully.

"Well, if you haven't got your finger ready, you can't shoot," the policeman noted helpfully.

Jack flushed, and adjusted his grip. "Okay. I'm ready now," he assured the man, and this time he really meant it. "What's the show?"

Darek squinted at the rearview mirror of a truck parked conveniently across the street. "One behind the desk. I'll handle him; you cover my back, just in case."

"Alright," the eighteen-year-old replied, affecting a small, brave smile.

Darek returned it easily. He was used to dangerous circumstances like the one they were in now. "Then let's go," he decided. He readied himself to step forward. "Three, two, one..."

CRASH! The glass in the gun shop door shattered as the Annapolis policeman shot through it at the Inter behind the counter; once, twice, thrice. His aim was so accurate that the second and third bullets passed through the hole the first one had made.

The Inter inside collapsed. Jack yanked the shop door open, and he and Darek ran in, setting off a Level 4 alarm—but they didn't care, as there was no countermeasure.

Jack pulled the counter drawer open and slammed his finger down on the purple button. The secret door behind him opened, and the two hurried down the steps, their guns at the ready. Time was of the essence.

* * *

"Why'd they have to have their generators near the waterfront?" Cloe was muttering. "We're going to get all wet if there's a fight."

"Not necessarily," Joyce countered. "But if there's a fight and we're losing, then we've got an alternate escape route. You *can* swim, right?"

"Of course I can," Cloe replied, sniffing disdainfully at what she considered an obvious question. Erin hid a smile.

"Well then, we'll be fine," Joyce surmised. She glanced ahead of them, through the darkening back street to the harbor. "Time to quiet down, now.

We'll be there in a few minutes."

* * *

Conner jogged down one of the Encephalon hallways, a relatively empty one. It hadn't been quite empty a few minutes before, but now it was, except for Conner—he'd dealt with the single guard there quietly and efficiently, as he'd been trained to do. He was somewhat surprised that there weren't more of them about, but this hallway, one of the ones that just happened to be closer to the high-tech stuff like the Schwann machine, didn't usually have whole crowds milling about, so he dismissed the thought.

Inter that he was, his bones ached almost painfully, which was why he wasn't running. He felt as if he'd smashed through a brick wall, which he had—but the feeling was going away fast. He quickened his pace, knowing it was only a matter of time before someone would see him and raise the alarm before he could silence them.

He was looking at the door numbers as he ran. He knew which door led to the Schwann room. He also knew that it was a highly guarded room, with special access codes and the like. He'd been in there before, with Trinity and Lyndon, and it just so happened that Conner had a good memory.

Especially now.

There it was, the door bare of any number or label. It was a very heavy looking door, made of some purple-tinted metal. It looked like it would be extremely hard to smash through.

Conner charged it, running at his top speed, which wasn't something to sneeze at. And the door more than sneezed; it shook violently, and nearly popped off the hinges. Conner retreated about a dozen feet, and went at it again, harder this time. And this time he—and his suit—succeeded.

The door fell inwards, hitting the ground with a terrific clang that echoed and re-echoed throughout the hall. Conner reflected grimly that he'd just raised the alarm, himself, but he didn't waste any time thinking about it, and darted forward, down the small hallway and into the safe-room.

There was no one in there. There wasn't usually, Conner knew. He flipped on the lights, hoisting his Violet Army rifle off his back and into a usable position. There it was: the metal box in the corner.

It looked harmless enough, but Conner knew that once it was destroyed the Violet Army would be destroyed as well, and possibly even himself.

He took a deep breath, holding his small yet powerful gun at arm's length. He forced himself to breathe out slowly, and then in again.

He didn't want to do this. But he had to.

He wished Moira were there with him now, just in case, but she couldn't have been, he realized. There was no other way.

He'd gotten this far, and he couldn't go back now. It was time to finish this, once and for all.

Conner lifted his gun, and braced himself. Then he started shooting.

forty-two

"Is that seriously all?" Jack had to ask, glancing down the short hallway.

"Looks like it," Darek grunted, reloading his gun quickly. He looked up, and gestured toward the first door on the right. "That's our first stop. Is it locked?"

Jack stepped over to the door, and twisted the knob. "No—"

The door flew open, hitting him in the face. Darek turned, and shot twice at the scientist who'd been trying to leave the room.

Jack fell back against the wall, and touched his nose gingerly. He tried not to look at the man on the ground, but still he felt like he might be sick.

The veteran policeman looked at him briefly. "You okay?"

"Yeah," Jack mumbled. He forced a small grin, and followed Darek into the first room of the Encephalon laboratory.

No one else was in there, and everything was neatly packed away in metal cabinets. Darek lifted his gun again.

"Got your earplugs in?" he asked Jack. The boy nodded, stepping behind him.

But then, before he could begin shooting, Darek felt the hairs on the back of his neck rise. He half-heard, half-felt the sudden draft from behind him, and he knew even before he turned around that there was a wall panel there, and that it had slid open. He and Jack turned at the same instant, Darek keeping his gun at the ready.

A whole crowd of Inters stood there. Jack counted eleven, twelve... Twenty. And in front of them stood a tall, foreboding figure: Hilton Maughan.

All of them were dressed head-to-toe in their special, bulletproof suits.

Jack caught his breath.

Darek didn't even wait for them to speak before he started shooting, repeatedly, clenching his teeth and ignoring the kicks. It was useless. Slowly Darek dropped his arm to his side. Jack wanted to hide behind him, but he managed to stay where he was. He fought not to let his terror show in his face, but still he was sweating. What was this?

"We've been waiting," Hilton greeted smoothly, smiling slightly. "Follow us, if you please," he added as his men surrounded the two and relieved them of their weapons. "We do have an appointment to keep. Glad you could make it."

Darek nodded briefly, his face hard and his jaw tight and tense. He didn't make to answer. He didn't need to.

* * *

"It's gone," Moira gasped about the same time. She looked quickly around the room, then back at the empty table. "This is the room. It's exactly like Conner said it was. But the Lens is gone!"

Her fellow hackers were already making themselves busy. Niamh was getting the computer in the room up and running, while Giulia ransacked the single cabinet.

"Some of the stuff is in here," she reported a moment later. "A box with headsets and microphones. But that's just backup. Looks like they've cleaned the place up." She added something in Italian. Moira didn't ask what she'd said; the vehement disgust in her voice was enough to get her meaning across.

"Then they knew we were coming," Moira breathed, still staring at the table that had held the complicated, powerful Lens radio at some point in the past. "That's why we didn't run into anyone on our way here."

"This thing is logged out," Niamh concluded a moment later, and stood up from the desk. She scowled hard at the useless computer, fighting the urge to smash it in her frustration.

"What do we do?" Moira asked the adults quietly. But her mind was busy running through the implications of the Encephalon expecting their attack.

There was no way the Encephalon would have evacuated simply because they were going to be attacked. No. They had let them walk in. It had been a trap.

They would be captured any minute now. There were only seconds left. And everyone else—

"Niamh, Giulia," she whispered. Niamh glanced at the sixteen-year-old, and saw that her face was white. "We need to get everyone out of here now. If it isn't too late."

"It is," came a new voice from the doorway.

Niamh, Giulia, and Moira spun around. But they already knew what was coming.

* * *

Cloe was freaking out. She'd never been in the middle of a pitched battle before. But here she was, in the middle of one, in a dark back street with Violet Army Inters everywhere and shouts filling her ears, a fifteen-year-old girl. She was with Joyce and Erin; the Violet Army hadn't managed to separate the three. She wanted to do something to help. Erin and Joyce were fighting like the trained professionals they were, and covering her, Cloe.

But Cloe was just terrified stiff. Everything was dark, except for the headlights of the Inter suits, including Joyce's. The Inters weren't shooting, for fear they'd hit each other, but Joyce and Erin were firing into them. They were so closely surrounded that the two paratroopers didn't even have to take aim. Cloe realized that the Inters were more trying to take them prisoner than wipe them out.

One question filled her mind; everything else was a blur. Cloe felt that maybe the two adults were wondering the same thing: *When will Conner destroy the Schwann?*

"You can give up now," an Inter called. Or maybe it was their leader. "We were onto you from the start. Trooper A1 betrayed you."

And that sparked Cloe into action. She knew Conner. She had known him for years. And she knew he never would, never *could* do such a thing.

"Liar!" she screamed, finally discovering how to use her gun—by pulling the trigger, aiming in the general direction of the taunting voice. Nothing else changed, but she lost her paralysis, and continued to help her friends.

"Good!" Erin shouted to her, not unaware of the younger girl's efforts. Cloe managed a weak grin.

Joyce didn't make a comment. She was too busy fighting off a taller, stronger attacker—Reina Patterson. The Reflex officer knocked the gun away from the paratrooper, and brought up her own, targeting the light that glinted off Joyce's helmet visor. Undaunted, Joyce kicked the Reflex's gun away smoothly, then swayed forward to smash her gloved fist into Reina's helmet.

Reina's hand flew to her belt, and she brought it back up holding a small knife that glinted purple in the faint light. The blade wasn't metal, but some other material that Joyce couldn't quite identify in the moment before she swung her arms out in a slicing pattern, up and down and up and down, her personal tactic for dealing with knives. Reina wasn't expecting it, and held it in front of her defensively.

Joyce seized her chance to knock away the knife, but not before the strange blade bit deep, through the glove around her wrist and through the skin as well. She gasped as she felt a thick, cold liquid leak out of her suit and into the wound. There were a few seconds of severe, stinging pain, and then her hand and lower forearm went completely numb.

"Oh joy," Joyce hissed sharply, flexing her fingers. They curled once, twice, and then she lost control.

Her arm was freezing, and it was spreading. The Myelin had gotten into her bloodstream. She realized her cut wasn't even bleeding. Her entire hand was turning to ice. And it was spreading fast, up her arm. First the darts of stinging pain, then the dull numbness, then nothing.

She tore her glove off, ignoring the battle going on around her, and stared at her hand. It was turning a light purple-blue, her veins accentuated. She felt her breath coming quick and fast.

No. Was this going to kill her?

"Joyce!" Cloe was shouting, Joyce realized. "Are you okay?" The paratrooper looked down at the shorter Marwick girl. Cloe was staring at her anxiously. Reina had her by the shoulder, and Cloe was panting.

"Joyce!" Cloe shouted again, when she didn't get an answer.

The fifteen-year-old spun around and attacked Reina, getting in only a couple of useless hits before the Reflex angrily kicked her off balance. Joyce dimly sensed the girl scrambling around for something in the dirt, but then she heard Erin's sharp gasp from behind her. Nothing else, but Joyce knew it was over. Especially when Reina laughed, a chilling sound.

"Give up!" she ordered, just as someone finally got a light on. Joyce turned to see Cloe and Erin both being held tightly. As for herself, she was only dimly aware of the gun pointed at her back. The ice-feeling was spreading. She felt herself going into a state of shock.

"We're heading back to Encephalon." She could still hear Reina, albeit faintly. "And you—Erin French, I think? You'd better help your friend. The more she moves, the faster that thing is going to spread." Another short laugh. "Not like it makes much of a difference anyway."

She felt her best friend's arm slide around her shoulder.

Erin whispered to her, "Joyce? Are...are you okay?"

Joyce didn't answer. She couldn't. But she didn't want to. Everything was so cold. And then she realized, as her eyes closed of their own accord and she felt her pulse dropping, this was the end.

forty-three

Conner shot until his gun ran out of ammunition. He lowered his tired arm, puzzled as to why he could move it at all. But then he realized nothing had happened. It wasn't the Schwann.

It took a few seconds for that to sink in and for Conner to realize he wasn't about to freeze after all. But he didn't have much time to think before the situation changed, and he wasn't alone anymore. He knew it from the instant his keen ears picked up the sound of footsteps in the corridor, a sound amplified by the listening mechanism in his helmet.

He didn't turn around. He didn't have to. The heavy metal walls served as basic mirrors, though the picture they presented was slightly blurry.

Conner used it to watch silently as the Violet Army ranks oozed into the room, their guns at the ready. Conner counted them, and felt a weird sense of flattery that there were over fifteen there, just to deal with him, a sixteen-year-old renegade Inter.

He could recognize their leader when the Reflex officer stepped closer. It was his old comrade, Louis Staunton, the third of Trinity's bodyguard trio—and Trooper's rival.

Louis didn't stop until he was only a couple of feet behind the younger Inter, and the end of his gun rested directly on the back of Conner's collar.

Conner felt a strange sense of something almost like calm. He'd never been in a scenario like this, with death literally right behind him, and now that he was, he was shocked at how unafraid he felt. Maybe it was because of the fact that Joyce had modified his collar, though he doubted it would stand up to a direct bullet.

"Good to see you back, A1," Louis told him in a voice filled with contempt.

Conner shrugged easily. "Is it really?" he asked, swinging around suddenly and using his gun to smash Louis over the head at the same time as he kicked him, hard. Louis stumbled back, dazed. The other Inters crowded around Conner, surrounding him. The boy laughed recklessly.

"I can take on all of you at once," he shouted, remembering the day he had woken up and been forced to "fight." He had survived a fight against twenty soldiers, and that was before Trinity had trained him.

They stared back at him, their faces expressionless. Conner had half a moment to catch his breath. Then one of the Inters started the contest by attacking him from the back.

A pitched battle followed. Conner held his own. But eventually the strain began to tell.

The men he had fought for Lyndon had not been superhuman, and these were. He was stunning a few of them, but he doubted his success would last long, and meanwhile the others just tried harder.

It began to tell, all too soon. Conner forgot about winning and started to make his way to the door. He bet he could run faster than any of them, and hopefully find out what was going on with Moira. But the Violet Army were everywhere, pounding away and landing hits that even the Myelin couldn't quite absorb. Conner could see why Trinity and Lyndon had insisted on intense physical training and not just aim and trajectory angles.

He started breathing faster, in ragged gasps, as he fought back now with a new, desperate strength. He was getting bruises all over, and now it hurt to fight. He didn't want to fight anymore, but the hope of helping Moira and his friends kept him going.

Then someone hit him from behind, a blow full of fury and powerful strength. Conner staggered for only a moment, but it was too long. His new attacker hit him again, and again. Conner bent double, then collapsed forward on his face, landing painfully on the concrete floor. Someone kicked him over, and he looked up, straight into the dark and angry face of Louis Staunton.

"Get up," the man barked out through clenched teeth. "And get moving," he added as Conner pulled himself up, exhausted and beaten.

The remaining Inters surrounded the sixteen-year-old, and pushed him to begin walking.

"I'm going to kill you," Conner heard Louis hiss. "Just as soon as Trinity gives the word. I will. I swear."

Conner didn't feel like answering, so he didn't bother.

He was so tired, he thought ruefully as they led him out of the room and across the hall, then down some stairs and through another hall. They walked a good distance, and Conner was pleased to note he was regaining his strength quickly.

But then it seemed they'd arrived.

They shoved him into a room, and he stared aghast at his friends, including Nina, arrayed against the far wall, each of them held at gunpoint, except Joyce. The paratrooper was leaning on Erin, and there was something strange about her.

As Conner looked harder, he realized what it was: there was an icy, frozen look to her pale blue face that made him catch his breath. Her sleeve was cut, and there were a few drips of some frosty blue ice on her suit. He realized right away what had happened, and he bit his lip.

He leaned against the wall next to her, letting his customary strength flow back to him gradually, and felt Moira's hand slip into his gloved one. He didn't look back at her, not trusting himself to be able to handle it, but he did squeeze back. Whatever happened next, they would be facing it together.

Watching the Violet Army soldiers at the other side of the room, Conner surmised that they were waiting for someone; probably Trinity, he decided. All they were really doing was blocking the doorway. And now that all ten of them were there, the soldiers closer to them headed back to be with the others.

Conner sensed Louis's dark stare for a moment, and he looked up, but the Reflex had turned his attention to Joyce. He was staring hard at the American paratrooper, and Conner hadn't the foggiest idea why.

But as he'd glanced at Joyce, himself, he realized that they had to do something. And immediately. Nina was already edging cautiously over to the paratrooper.

"She needs a blood transfusion," he whispered to the paramedic.

Nina glanced at him for a moment before a look of understanding crossing her face.

"And T4," Conner added. "What blood type is she?"

"Huh?" Nina blinked. "I dunno."

"Type O," Erin supplied from a few feet away. She was next to her friend. "O negative."

"Oh heavens," Conner whispered.

"That's the rarest," Nina muttered.

Conner bit his lip till he tasted blood. "I know." He paused. "I'm B, so we don't match. I could give her some for the T4, but her blood would reject it. Oh, I don't know..." He wrung his hands. "Why does she have to be O? Does anyone else have O?"

There was a chorus of quiet "No's" down the line. Conner caught his breath and glanced back at the Violet Army soldiers, but they didn't seem to care that the prisoners were talking.

"Does that mean we can't save her, then?" Erin whispered, a hint of panic in her voice.

"I'm thinking—I know I've seen it before—" Conner began, but then he banged the back of his head on the wall behind him violently. "Oh joy. Of all the people!"

"Who?" Erin queried tentatively, turning to look at the boy.

He pointed briefly, then lifted his free hand to rub the back of his helmet instinctively in an effort to comfort his skull after accidentally bashing it against a bulletproof helmet. He'd pointed at the tall figure who was now entering the room. "*Her*, of course. Who else?"

forty-four

It was Trinity.

She was wearing her purple jacket as usual, Conner noted. And her short skirt and tights and boots. With a small, almost innocently happy smile on her face. Conner knew that smile. It was the congrats-that-was-amazing smile.

Hilton Maughan, Lyndon's right-hand man, was there, too, as were Reina Patterson and Louis Staunton. The four were backed by Inters, so many of them that some stood waiting in the hallway. It was obvious that they had a job to do, and just as obvious what that job was.

Conner felt an uneasy twinge, just as he saw out of the corner of his eye that Cloe was passing something to Jack from her bleeding hand. He wondered abstractly what it was.

But he was still watching Trinity, out of eyes weary and somewhat sad, yet still irrefutably alive. She looked at him, too, for an instant; but then she lost her smile, and glanced over at Hilton.

The officer had been waiting for her signal to begin, and now he began to speak. "Well, then, now that we're all here, I think it's time to finish this."

He looked tentatively over at Louis Staunton, who nodded urgently. "Staunton?"

"Yes sir," Louis returned, saluting.

"You and your men may begin," Hilton ordered calmly. Conner stared in cold horror at the smile of evil delight that came on Louis's face. But then Trinity's clear, girlish voice interrupted the whole process.

"Wait. I've changed my mind."

Everyone, including Hilton, turned to look at her in surprise. She hadn't spoken at all yet, but now she was leaning against the wall, staring at Conner.

"Don't kill A1," she decided, and Conner froze. "Nor Moira Whyte, nor Clotilde Marwick."

"Trinity Ryder, your father said—" Hilton began uneasily.

Trinity dismissed the warning with a spasmodic wave of her gloved hand. "Not right now, Maughan. Dad will be okay with it. We just need Clotilde and Moira for a while, and then you're going to help me fix up A1—"

"No," Conner interrupted. "I'm not going back, Trinity." His jaw was tight.

Trinity's eyebrows shot up. "Oh? What makes you think you have a choice? Either you and the other two come with us peacefully, or the rest will go long and slow, like—"

She paused momentarily, a pause full of meaning. "Like Joyce Liszt over there."

Conner glanced at the paratrooper, and then back at the Violet Army leader, his eyes pleading. "Trinity, you can't let her die like that. Are you O-negative?"

"What?" Trinity was momentarily taken aback.

"O-negative. I know you are, I've seen your charts," Conner answered his own question. "You're the only one who can save her, Trin. You have to, or she'll die soon. She needs a transfusion. And T4. You have both. You *have* to save her, Trin!"

There was a second of silence, then Reina started muttering something angrily. But it turned out she didn't have to worry, because Trinity's seeming lack of response was due only to disbelieving surprise that someone would ask her such a thing.

"Are you *kidding* me?" she asked incredulously. "No, I don't have to, and I'm not going to. What do you take me for, your secret ally?"

Snickers along the Inter line. Reina's mouth relaxed into a smug smile.

Conner shook his head, but Trinity didn't wait for him to further his case. "Anyway. Let's get going."

"No," Conner said again, "because if you don't save Joyce, right now, and tell your men not to hurt anybody, then you get—" He paused to catch his breath.

"Well?" Trinity queried curiously.

"Then you get nothing." He clenched his fists, breathing out slowly. "Nothing and nobody at all."

Trinity shrugged. "We'll see," she returned, and gestured to Reina. In turn, Reina signaled to a couple of her soldiers, and they walked the pace of the room, stopping directly in front of Conner, who braced himself to tackle both of them.

But then they did something utterly unexpected: one jerked Moira away from her twin, and the other pulled out a syringe.

"Get away from her!" Conner shouted as Moira screamed her twin's name and went into dead weight mode, dropping on the floor.

Conner jumped on the Inter with the tranquilizer syringe; suddenly an idea struck him, and he grabbed the solution-tipped syringe just before it shattered on the concrete floor.

He smashed the soldier's helmet into the floor with his free hand, and then left him there, stunned, and jumped up to deal with the second soldier, who was starting to drag Moira off, despite her tactic of lying limp. Conner pounced on him from behind, making him let go of Moira at the same time as holding the tranquilizer, somehow without crushing it in his hand.

Moira rolled away and scrambled to her feet with Giulia's help, and Conner tangled with the soldier. They both ended up on the ground, and after a few seconds Conner found himself underneath, kicking desperately as he tried to keep the syringe away from his antagonist. Then he felt an added weight as someone leapt onto the pile, shouting to Conner to flip the tables.

Conner took the suggestion literally, summoning a mighty effort and rolling over. The enemy soldier landed on the ground, with Jack on top of him.

Conner was about to help out, but then he realized Jack had the advantage, with some knife he knew to be of the same design as what they used to deal with G-fiber. He didn't waste any time trying to figure out how Jack had gotten the knife, but he spun around in the instant of respite and passed Erin the syringe. She was closest.

"I fear a general without an army, but not an army without a general,"

Conner quoted Napoleon, perhaps without realizing it.

Erin nodded seriously, understanding his meaning, and Conner turned around to deal with the Inters that now ran up. He threw them back with renewed strength, strength replenished and increased because now he fought to protect not only himself but his sister and friends as well.

All hell broke loose then, Conner and his friends knowing instinctively that it was the final battle between the opposing forces, and that only one could win, and that one would win forever.

Both were equally determined to win. The Violet Army was impatient to finish this, once and for all. And the ten, the remaining nine of the ten, were equally desperate to save their lives, their homes, their America—the world. There would be no more fighting. Only death and defeat—or victory and glory.

Darek, Niamh, and Giulia were protecting themselves as well as the Marwick girls, and doing a good job of it, too. Moira commandeered some of the fallen Inters' guns, passed a few of them to Darek, Giulia, and Niamh, and kept the last one for herself. Meanwhile Conner, Erin, and Jack were trying to clear a way to the Violet Army leaders through the soldiers that now flooded the room.

Conner knew that they were by the door, and he knew they only had a short time before Reina and Louis would notice that the nine were winning—if things turned out that way—and get Trinity out of there. His arms moved like windmills as he plowed away to let Erin get through.

The paratrooper fought with a strength and passion she didn't know she'd had before. She felt almost like her friend's emergency had become her own, and now she surpassed herself in her efforts to win. To survive.

Jack was using the knife Cloe had passed to him, marveling at its seeming ease to pierce the supposedly strong G-fiber. He had never fought like this before, but there was no backing down now, and besides both of his older and younger sisters depended on their winning this battle.

He was covering Erin's and Conner's backs, merely following where they went. Together the three worked as a single machine, accomplishing feats they could never have achieved on their own.

They were getting closer to their goal. Conner lost some of his caution in his haste, and Jack suddenly saw one of the officers—Louis Staunton—plunging for the boy with his own knife.

The thought crossed Jack's mind that probably only the officers had these special knives, most likely to enable them to deal with mutinies. But Conner was unaware of his new attacker, and Jack leapt into action to save his friend.

Literally.

He tackled Louis with one flying leap, bringing him to the ground just inches away from Conner's suit. His knife clattered away from him on the floor, but so did Louis's.

Louis turned his attention away from Conner for the moment, with eighteen-year-old Jack clinging tightly to his back, and devoted his formidable energies to giving the unprotected teenager a beating he would never forget.

Jack gasped, then yelled for help, just before Louis pulled his gun off his belt and finished the job. The cry ended abruptly, terminating with the echoes of the gunshot.

"Jack!" Conner screamed, forgetting about their mission, about Trinity, about everything except his friend's scream.

Turning, he flung the Reflex off his older friend, and shoved a few Inters away, dropping to his knees to look at Jack.

A moment of staring at his prostrate friend sufficed to tell him that it was already over.

Jack lay limply where he had fallen, his twisted face a pale, drained white. He was bleeding slowly where the bullet had gone in, unhampered not one bit by the coat he wore. His eyes stared blankly up at Conner, completely expressionless.

Conner felt his chest, hoping to find some signs of life. There were none.

The sixteen-year-old screamed again, this time wordlessly, a cry not unlike his a few days before when he had suddenly remembered. But even as he felt the first pangs of losing his best friend, Conner knew he could not give up now.

He had to keep fighting, and win—for Jack. He jumped up and struggled on twice as desperately, while tears stung his eyes, blinding him.

forty-five

Meanwhile, Trinity and Hilton were making their way over to the door, Hilton mentally ranting about how none of this would be happening if Trinity hadn't had to be so adamant about making her own decisions.

Erin looked up and saw they were leaving and that Trinity's back was turned. She realized this was her only chance.

She dodged a rifle and ran ahead, ducking to avoid other blows as she caught up to Trinity. Hilton turned, and saw Erin just as she came even with the two. He opened his mouth to warn the Violet Army leader, but Erin was already jerking the needle out of the tiny-dose canister and jabbing it into Trinity's exposed wrist.

Trinity felt the sudden, almost imperceptible sting, and wheeled around to see who was there, but then she felt her arm numbing as Erin emptied the solution into her. She stared vacantly into the paratrooper's flaming blue eyes, feeling her senses gradually fading away from her.

"Thanks for saving Joyce," Trinity heard the Irish girl whisper angrily as everything went black.

* * *

She woke up a few minutes later, but everything was dark. People were shouting, and Reina was pulling the nineteen-year-old up to her feet. Trinity's head hurt, but she could feel the headache going away quickly.

"What happened?" she asked, in a voice quite annoyed, though she still felt a bit groggy.

There was a click, and Reina's flashlight turned on. "That Erin French injected you with the tranquilizer for the Whyte girl, and then suddenly the power cut."

She paused, shining the flashlight around the room. The beams played over the nearly deserted battlefield, and Trinity could see a few stunned Inters, as well as Jack's limp form. She stood up and felt her wrist where the needle had gone in.

"What's going on now?" she demanded.

"Louis is leading the others in pursuit," Reina supplied. "They won't get far."

"I'm going, too," Trinity decided suddenly, heading off in the direction of the doorway. She grabbed her gloves off her belt and pulled them on as she went, determined not to make the same mistake twice.

"Trin—wait—" Reina began, but the strong-willed teenager was already gone.

***

Trinity was running down the dark corridor. She heard shouts, yells, and gunshots. They told her that she was going in the right direction.

Presently she made a turn, almost directly into the scene of a desperate last stand. Only a few flashlights pierced the darkness, mostly from Inter helmets, and she could see Conner farther down, blocking the hallway. She understood right away what was happening. He was holding them off so that the others could escape in the sudden power outage.

He was doing a good job of it, too. Even alone he was winning. Only so many Inters could crowd into the hallway at a time, and Conner made full use of the different techniques and tricks Trinity had taught him. The others would get away, Trinity realized, unless they got past him somehow, and immediately.

She sighed without noticing it as she pulled out her own gun for the first time that evening. She hadn't really wanted to use it, she realized subconsciously, but now it looked like she had to.

Only she could make a difference here. Because the suits had an intentional flaw, and only Trinity and her father knew about it.

Taking careful aim, Trinity paused a moment before firing to watch the target. He nearly went down under a sudden charge, and for a second or two disappeared from view, but then she could see him again.

The Inters fell back somewhat, and Trinity got a clear line of fire. Conner looked up. His visor was streaked with blood, and for an instant Trinity wondered whose it was. But most of it was clear, and she could see his face.

Suddenly she saw that he was looking straight at her. Almost blindly, as if he were still under the LVED. But his tired eyes were still alive, and he stared back at her.

She moved her index finger from the guard to the trigger, willing her hand to stop trembling—possibly a side effect of the tranquilizer.

So many different things were in her mind at that instant that she never knew afterward what she was primarily thinking. There was annoyance that they'd in part succeeded, in literally stealing blood to save Joyce Liszt. But there was also honest admiration for that; it was something Trinity had to admit she would have done herself. There was a tinge of victory; if she fired this shot, they would win. There was also disappointment that it was over so soon, a reluctance to fire that final shot.

She felt sorry for Conner, or Trooper, she realized. She always had. As a puny kid up against odds he could never realize. As the robot soldier, forced to obey every command, despite whatever he might really be thinking. As the prisoner, tormented by the thought that he had shot his own sister. And as the enemy soldier, fighting those he had once known as somewhat "friends," desperate to protect those whom he loved.

She had seen him as all four. But what really slowed her shot here was the fact that the Inter had saved her life. It had been completely unexpected, completely unasked for. But if he hadn't done what he'd done, then she might not be here now.

They believed in what they were fighting for. And it really was something worth fighting for, Trinity realized. Country, home, family, all in one.

They didn't share any of the high, far-fetched ideas of Lyndon and his daughter. No, they believed in what they knew to be possible, and what they knew to be good and true. And here they were, fighting for it.

And here they were, dying for it.

Trinity's mind went blank. Could she really bear to end this dream of love and peace and happiness forever?

And then she knew she couldn't do it. Slowly, as if in a dream, she dropped her arm to her side. And then she saw that Conner was finally going down, and she screamed out one word, in a voice cracking, yet somehow powerful enough to be heard throughout the hall.

"STOP!"

She saw the soldiers turn to stare at her, shocked.

Conner stumbled back, looking stunned.

Puzzled, Hilton came over to Trinity. "Tri—"

"Shut up," she hissed, loudly enough for everyone to hear. "Not another word. I'm finished," she added, a curious tone creeping into her voice. "I'm finished with it all. You guys can keep fighting if you like. I don't care. But I'm joining Trooper."

Hilton's mouth dropped open in speechless surprise. He literally couldn't say a word. But Trinity was finished.

She walked slowly down the hall, replacing her gun in her belt as she went. The soldiers parted to make way for her as she neared the tired, exhausted soldier. Conner was still leaning against the wall, breathing heavily, his eyes closed. But then she stood in front of him.

"Conner Whyte," she spoke firmly, and he opened his eyes. "I apologize. I know you wouldn't join us, and I know why. But will you and your friends accept me?" she asked quietly. And she held out her purple-gloved hand.

Conner stared at it for a moment before reaching out and shaking it. He didn't smile. He was too shaken after losing his friend Jack. But he did shake her hand.

"I'm sure we'll be glad to have you, Trinity Ryder. And I'll try to forgive you."

She shook her head. "No. I said I'm finished. My name is Violet Arnnu," she insisted.

He nodded. "Violet Arnnu, then. Welcome... Vi."

forty-six

"Let me go help him!" Moira was screaming. She fought Giulia's strong grip with a young wildcat's strength. "They're going to kill Conner!"

"Just stop," the energetic Italian returned, maintaining her grip on Moira's shoulder nonetheless. "You're going to get yourself killed, and where would Conner be then, eh?"

"Let me go," Moira repeated, as suddenly an idea came to her. She tried the same twist she'd once taught Conner and finally managed to break free.

They were far out of sight now, with Joyce and the syringe of blood Erin had gotten from Trinity, and Giulia was impatient to join them. Conner had intended to hold back their enemies so they could escape. But things weren't working that way, it seemed, and it was all the impetuous Moira's fault.

"Get back here!" Giulia yelled, with an addition in Italian, and stamped her foot. It was useless. Sighing, she started running after Moira. She'd said she would look after her, and Giulia was no shirker.

Meanwhile, Moira was running as well, back to the faint sounds of battle. Her long brunette hair flew out behind her as she tore down the hallway. She felt her heart sink as suddenly the shouting and shooting stopped, and she could hear nothing. She stopped and leaned against the wall, panting slightly. Did the silence mean that the Violet Army had won?

She bit her lip, struggling against panic. They couldn't have won. If they had, she would be hearing something besides silence. So something else was happening.

Slightly heartened by that, Moira started running again, faster. She heard voices now, just around the corner ahead of her. She turned it—and ran slap-bang into her twin.

Had he been as frail as he used to be, the collision would probably have ended with both of them on the floor, but as it was, Conner regained balance almost immediately, and caught Moira before she fell. The twins hugged, and Moira was so relieved at finding Conner safe and sound that she started crying before she could control herself.

"You're safe!" she choked out, feeling as if now everything would be all right.

"I dunno about that yet, if people are gonna keep running into me," Conner murmured ironically, gently helping her stand up on her own. "But I'm glad you're okay. Where is everyone else?" he asked, looking ahead and only seeing Giulia, who now slowed to a walk. "Also, we have an ally."

Moira glanced past him and noticed Violet for the first time, standing a distance behind Conner and watching quietly. The sixteen-year-old froze, and stared.

"Trinity Ryder?" she asked Conner incredulously.

Violet shook her head, smiling slowly, and walked closer to join them. "No, Violet. Violet Arnnu."

Moira stepped back from her twin, shaking her head in disbelief.

"You're kidding," she told him, still staring at Violet, who stared back.

Conner shook his head seriously. "No, I'm not."

"What the—?" Giulia demanded, coming even with the other three.

"I want to join you," Violet told the older adult. "I'm finished with the Violet Army. If you guys will have me—" She paused meaningfully.

Moira turned to Conner. "How can you trust her?" she demanded, her voice rising in shock and skepticism. "Conner, she's—"

"Vi may be a murderer and a criminal, but she isn't a liar," Conner told his twin softly.

"Look, Conner, she and her dad turned you into a monster. And she was going to do it again!" Moira felt frustration rising. "And what about Jack? Are you just gonna—"

"Moira," Conner interrupted, his dark blue eyes pleading with her. "I know what you mean. But does Jack want us, and America, to lose?"

"I say she's fine," Giulia said suddenly. Moira wheeled around to look at her, aghast.

"Violet, Conner, Moira." The insightful Italian managed a smile. "Let's go catch up to the others, shall we?"

The four set off down the hall, Violet and Giulia slightly in advance of the twins; Conner was tired, and Moira wanted to walk with him. Plus she was horrified at Giulia's acceptance of Violet.

"I can't believe you two," she was whispering to Conner. "How?"

Conner shrugged uneasily. "Sometimes things have to be done, even if you don't like to do them."

"But letting Violet work with us is like betraying everything we're fighting for!" Moira reminded him.

"You know what?" Conner had to ask. "She's joining us, not the other way around. And that actually destroys the basis of the Violet Army. With Vi on our side, the war is over," he finished, his eyes alight with victory.

"Huh?" Moira was confused. She didn't know the workings at Encephalon as well as Conner did.

He managed a weak, grim smile. "Because Lyndon started this war for his daughter, and he's not going to fight her. You'll see."

Moira heaved a long, drawn-out sigh. "Okay then. As long as you trust her. Because I trust you," she added, glancing up at him.

"I trust her." He smiled down at her. "And I'll take care of you either way. Satisfied? Let's stop arguing."

She nodded, and slipped her hand into his. "Okay."

forty-seven

But a week or so later they were arguing again; this time about something that might have seemed less important for some but for them was just as crucial.

The two were shoveling snow off the Whyte home driveway, a highly enjoyable activity for Conner, who used to hate such exertions but now took pleasure in them as opportunities to stretch and work out. Moira kept up with him dutifully, though it was to be doubted whether Conner was working as fast and hard as he might have been.

"Mom said she liked pink best the last time I asked her," Moira insisted, pausing with the shovel for a moment so she could brush a lump of snow off Conner's old coat, now irrefutably hers. "She did, I'm sure."

"No, she said yellow," Conner contradicted. "Remember how Dad got her yellow tulips for her birthday last spring?"

"They were more white than yellow." Moira shook her head. "And that's because they were out of pink. Dad said so."

"Yeah, well, Mom loved them," Conner pointed out dryly. "And we have more yellow paper than pink paper."

"You guys should just do a mix," came a new voice from behind them. The twins knew who it was, and Conner turned to greet the newcomer, while Moira scowled and shoveled harder.

"Hey, Vi." Conner waved with his shovel-free hand.

Violet had trimmed her bangs and cut her hair, and now her hair was plain dark brown without purple-dyed tips, but she still looked enough like herself, wearing her favorite, purple sweater. She had both hands stuck in her pockets, and was watching the twins amusedly.

"Hey, Conner, Moira," she returned, ignoring the fact that Moira hadn't welcomed her. "I decided to come early," she explained, smiling. A small layer of snow was gathering on her head and shoulders, and she shook herself momentarily to brush it off.

"Cool," Conner grinned. "We're just cleaning the driveway."

"I can help," Violet offered, stepping forward. "Actually Darek and Niamh want your help finishing up. We went through a couple of the labs together but they suggested I should probably get you to take my place, seeing as you... Uhh..." She broke off, and Moira turned to see a slight pink flush creeping into her cheeks.

"Oh, sure," Conner nodded. He dropped his shovel in a pile of snow to the side of the driveway, and it stayed standing upright. "Where are they now?"

Violet released her held breath, forming crystals in the crisp December air. "Rendezvous at Giulia's place—the one she's remodeling. Pervitto's." She remembered the name Giulia had decided on, and her eyebrows went up slightly. Conner laughed.

"Are they going to be done in time for the dinner?" Moira asked worriedly.

Violet nodded. "Yeah, Niamh said she wouldn't miss it for anything, and Darek is eager to finish. It'll be fine," she assured the younger girl. Moira's frown softened into a semi-smile.

"Well, you'll help Moira finish getting ready for dinner, won't you?" Conner demanded before starting to run. Running was his favorite way of getting places; the motorcycle he'd kept after the chaotic American victory, now stored safely away in the Whytes' garage, most definitely attracted attention. Especially now that the Annapolis population wasn't on LVED any longer.

"Sure!" Violet agreed. Her purple eyes twinkled as she watched Conner salute teasingly and then run off. Her smile faded, and she sighed subconsciously when she turned to look at Moira. She knew that the younger girl still didn't trust her, or didn't like her, or both. But Violet affected another, fake smile.

"Want help with anything?" she asked the sixteen-year-old.

Moira turned her attention back to shoveling snow industriously. "I guess," she replied without looking at Violet. "If you can stick the dinner in the oven that would be nice. It's in the fridge—the big casserole dish on the top shelf—350°, thirty minutes." She hesitated. "What time is it?"

Violet checked her watch. "Almost six."

Moira groaned. "Oh, only half an hour left then. Okay then, I'll see you later," she decided. But then she stopped shoveling snow. There was a determined air about her as she turned around, just as Violet was about to head inside. "Oh, and Tri—Violet?" she asked, suddenly losing her confident air.

Violet turned to her, surprised. "Yeah?"

Swallowing uncomfortably, Moira managed a small smile. "I just thought I should say thanks for joining us." Violet's purple eyes lit up, but Moira hadn't finished. "And sorry I've been so rude and unwelcoming," she continued softly with her apology. "I guess I just—"

"No, if anyone should say sorry, it's me," Violet interrupted her quickly. "I'm glad you got your brother back. I—"

Moira smiled faintly. "I know, right?"

"I'm sorry," Violet told her again, her voice slowly getting stronger. "I have no excuse. I'm sorry."

Moira nodded, her deep blue eyes meeting Violet's purple ones. "I forgive you. As long as I get to keep my brother."

A nervous laugh from the older girl. "Hey, I—"

"I'm joking," Moira amended.

Violet gave a timid smile. "Does this mean we're friends, Moira?"

"Mhmm. If you want to be," Moira added.

"Totally," Violet agreed. She giggled awkwardly.

"But I'm not done out here yet," Moira noted, looking back at the snow. "Do you wanna put dinner in the oven? I'll be in within five minutes," she promised rashly, tackling the remaining section of the driveway with renewed energy.

Violet nodded, skipping up the driveway, through the uncleared snow, and up the steps. She wrapped her fingers around the doorknob and pulled the door open, feeling the brief outrush of warm air from the house. Stepping inside, she scuffed her boots on the doormat, and headed tentatively down the tiny hall. She hadn't been here before.

She opened the first door to her left, but shut it almost instantly. The entire room spoke Moira's atmosphere, from the fluffy pink pillow on the bed to the coding chart taped up over the desk. It was definitely Moira's bedroom, Violet decided, and skipped the next door, assuming it would be Conner's room. At the end of the hallway she discovered the homey living room, and from living room, the kitchen, dining room, etc.

She found the casserole dish, and stuck it in the oven, struggling to figure out the controls for a moment but then succeeding. She debated whether she should go ask Moira what to do next or just stay inside. Probably stay inside, she decided, since Moira had said she wouldn't be long.

The nineteen-year-old pulled out a chair at the sideboard, and sat down, staring around the pleasant-looking kitchen. She fell to thinking.

The dinner-slash-party in half an hour was to welcome Mrs. Victoria Whyte back home. A lot of people would be there: Darek Lasek, Giulia Pervitto, Niamh and Erin French, Joyce Liszt, Cloe, Nina, and herself, as well as the Marwick parents, the Whytes' cousins, and Moira's friend Lucinda.

Violet smiled when she remembered how she'd met Lucinda Montoya, and Conner's cousins Percy, Mark, and Lila. It turned out that they'd been the ones to disable the generators, while the Encephalon were off their guard. Though they hadn't been involved, most of the time, they'd ended up saving the day.

And Joyce had gotten better, much to Erin's relief, even if she was a superhuman as well now. It turned out she liked it, and so did the U.S. Marines leaders, though Joyce wasn't really supportive of the tentative plan to inject the entire U.S. army with T4. But neither was the President, so it was hoped that the plan would fail.

Nina and Cloe and their parents would be wearing black, Violet speculated. She wondered if Nina's arm would be out of the sling yet. And wondering about that turned her thoughts back to her own past.

She remembered her father, and her face drooped. He was in prison now, after he'd taken all the blame upon himself to save Violet. She hoped they would let him go someday—after all, he'd done it for her. But the chances were slim. He and most of the other members of the Violet Army were awaiting trial. Violet sighed wistfully.

She would've been in prison herself, if it hadn't been for Lyndon. He had told the authorities that Violet was only involved because she was his daughter. And when that was coupled with the fact that she had defected and ended the war, arranging herself with the U.S. forces and literally retaking over three of the states for them, they let her off. So she was free.

Looking around the casual-style kitchen, she found herself wishing she'd had a childhood like this. With a sibling or two...With a real home. She knew that once there had been... But no. She did not like to remember that.

Her hands slipped into her pockets again, and she felt their contents pensively. She was glad to be done with all the Encephalon business, though some of it still remained with her, and would forever, she thought to herself wryly. But like Lyndon had said, she could write her own future, and she was liking it so far.

She was anxious to meet Mrs. Whyte. Everyone who knew her and had talked to Violet about her had said she was a very nice lady. Violet heard she'd been in the hospital in a coma since after Conner had gone missing. She stifled a giggle at the thought of the reaction Mrs. Whyte would probably have to seeing her youngest son back again, and stronger and taller than ever.

Violet didn't notice as the remaining minutes flew by, till she heard voices in the living room. She perked up, and checked her watch; it was a few minutes short of six-thirty. She could hear the voices. There were Moira's excited, happy tones, and Conner's deeper ones. Then Darek's, the deepest of all. Giulia's Italian-accented, chirpy voice, and Erin's and Niamh's slight Irish accents. Joyce's strong, Texas-style American. The Montoyas' characteristic light tones, and the Marwicks' ironic ones. Percy and Mark Smyth's sarcastic voices mixing with their younger sister Lila's cheerfully spoken words. And a new voice, one she hadn't heard before, uttering happy and startled exclamations of delight.

Violet slipped down from the stool, noticing that the timer on the oven read only a few more seconds. Flipping herself over to it superhumanly, she turned off the timer just before it would go off. She pulled on oven mitts from the drawer next to it, and retrieved the macaroni and cheese from the oven, leaving it on the stove to cool.

The dinner was ready. Violet tiptoed over to the doorway to the living room, pausing with her hand on the doorknob.

All the voices mingled together, and suddenly Violet felt overwhelmed.

They were all so friendly and happy. Surely she didn't belong here. Or did she?

But someone had already seen her, and pulled the door open, introducing her to the assembly. They turned to look at her, but Violet glanced first at the one who'd opened the door, the one she knew best out of all of them.

Their eyes met, and Violet smiled.

THE END

epilogue

The Encephalon Center 01 had long been deserted and was now abandoned to the underground creatures, who had made it their new favorite haunt. But now rats, spiders, and worms quickly retreated from the light that invaded their expansive home as footsteps sounded on the steep stairs for the first time in over fifteen years.

The steps creaked under the intruder's weight as he carefully made his way down, using a flashlight. He was tall, with dark brown hair and a hard-set jaw. His eyes were a dark gray, but something unusual burned in them, something that would have made any ordinary person start back in surprise. But he was alone.

He went cautiously through the hallway, pausing at the first door on the right and opening it only to see a scene of broken glass and purple stains. He muttered something in his disappointment, closed the door again, and went on.

He didn't open any of the other doors in that hallway, nor did he stop walking for several minutes. At last he seemed to find what he was looking for, and he stepped through the open doorway of a large room that looked like it had once been a battleground.

There were bullet holes in the ceiling, and in the walls, and in the floor. There was also a dark brown stain on a certain section of the floor, as well as various pieces of plastic and metal scattered about.

But the man was only interested in a small something that glinted dimly as he played his flashlight over it.

He stooped and picked it up, disengaging it easily from the cobwebs that bound it to the floor. He blew the first layer of dust off it and wiped it carefully on his pants before looking at it again, this time with the flashlight.

This time the object's nature was clear enough: a sharp blade of some purple-tinted crystal, beginning with a steel handle, and ending in a fine, slightly curved, lethal point. The man held it up to the light, watching it shine as a similar light glowed in his own eyes.

"Finally," he whispered, the first words to be heard in that room for years. "Finally. It's time for revenge."

About the Author

Gabrielle Marie Kozak is an American author whose fiction explores pressure, endurance, and the cost of refusing to surrender oneself to oppressive systems. Her debut, *The Trooper Series*, began as a body of work written before she graduated high school and introduced her recurring focus on individual sovereignty under strain.

The eldest of nine children, Gabrielle spent nearly two years as a religious sister before turning her attention fully to writing and publishing. Her stories center on those who carry responsibility, those who break beneath it, and those who survive when systems fail.

She lives in Nebraska and loves writing, coffee, and all things Poland.

Website: **gmariaek.com**

Also by Gabrielle Marie Kozak

Thank you for reading!

If this story stayed with you, I would be grateful if you'd consider leaving a short review. Reviews help books like this find the readers who need them.

Your time, your attention, and your support truly matter.

If you'd like to continue reading my work, **The Trooper Series** is the best place to start.

Trooper A2: "Little Trooper"

HE WAS RAISED TO BE SAFE. HE WAS BORN TO BE SOMETHING ELSE.

When **Evolet Whyte** first meets his real parents and siblings, they **shatter** his view on life–forever. **His mother has a story.** Does he trust her–or does he believe what **history itself** tells him?

The **truth won't wait** for him to find it in the skyscrapers and the classrooms. It's coming to find him–and it could d**estroy** both Evolet and his new-found family.

To survive, Evolet must **discover and awaken** the "Little" Trooper within.

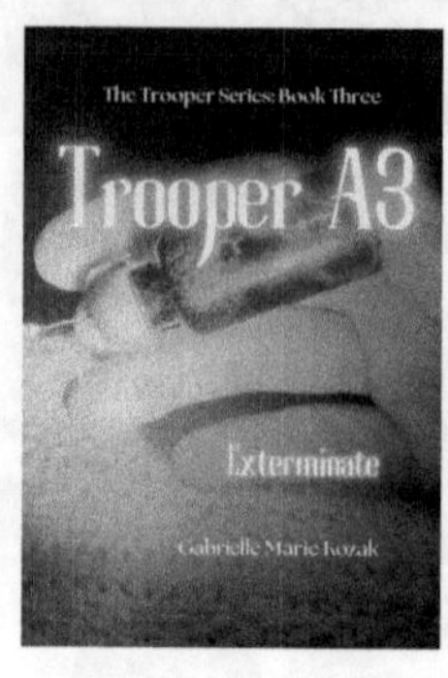

Trooper A3: Exterminate

SHE DIDN'T CHOOSE MOTHERHOOD—BUT RESPONSIBILITY CHOSE HER.

From a **college campus** to a **Texan laboratory**, Jasmine Whyte is beginning to realize that her **adult life** isn't going to be the peaceful future she fought for as a teenager. **Old ghosts** and **new threats** would like nothing better than to **tear her** from **her dreams**—and **her family.**

Jasmine isn't a mother. But there are children who **need her help.**

And she can only help them by letting them into her **own broken life**.

www.ingramcontent.com/pod-product-compliance
Lightning Source LLC
Chambersburg PA
CBHW060837080726
47818CB00042B/650

* 9 7 8 1 9 7 0 9 3 6 0 0 1 *